Signed Books and more

www.mattshawpublications.co.uk

How Much To..?

Matt Shaw

With Thanks to the following BETA readers:

Katie Bruce

Michael Cushing

Rowland Bercy

P. Muscutt

Melissa Potter

Unnecessary Introductions

Steven Gibson walked into the office kitchen area; a small room set aside for staff to enjoy a quiet break. He ignored the gentleman sitting at the table in the corner of the room and headed straight towards the freshly brewed coffee pot. It was a little before eight in the morning and, until he'd had his caffeine fix, he refused to talk to anyone.

The second man watched Steven as he quietly sipped at his own black coffee. Unlike Steven, it was his first day on the job and he still felt like a fish out of water. Watching Steven now, his mind was racing. Was he supposed to introduce himself? Was it better if Steven introduced himself first? Not that Nate Stephenson needed an introduction from the man he was replacing.

Steven sighed as he poured the coffee into a mug he'd claimed as his own since first starting the job there. It was the biggest mug in the cupboard. There was nothing fancy about it. There was a chip on the rim, close to the handle and it was plain black; nothing fancy whatsoever but definitely the biggest one there and, therefore, capable of holding the most coffee. Steven had already decided that, when the clock struck 5pm, the mug would be coming with him.

With the mug full, he sat the coffee pot back down and, still with his back to Nate, took a slow sip. His senses rushed the moment the coffee passed his lips. A little sip of heaven, right there, even if the brew was no longer quite as fresh as it had been.

Unable to take the silence anymore, Nate said, 'It's not the best, is it?'

Steven visibly winced at the sound of Nate's voice. One sip of coffee did not make him sociable. Slowly he turned around to look at the man who had dared address him before he was ready. Just as Nate needed no introductions, neither did Steven. This was the guy he was supposed to be showing around and training up before leaving for greener pastures. Knowing they'd have a long day together, and it would be even longer if Steven didn't *try* and be sociable a little at least, he said, 'I have been here eight years. I can assure you, the coffee doesn't get much better than this. That's your first little tip of the day.'

'I'll keep that in mind.'

Steven walked over to the table and took a seat opposite Nate. 'You're Nate Stephenson.'

'I am.'

'And you know who I am?'

'Steven Gibson.'

'Well that's the introductions out of the way.'

'So today really is your last day?'

Steven nodded. 'Eight long years and finally leaving to follow my other passions. Sometimes you just have to take the plunge and if I don't do it now, I never will.'

'May I ask what you're going to be doing?'

Steven smiled. 'Management.'

'Management?'

'Music management.' Steven explained, 'I've worked my arse off here for eight years and the money isn't bad but, the real money? That's in the music industry.'

'Management?'

'Musicians come and go. One band comes, a manager is there to guide them. The band, singer, whatever...

They have their day and the listeners move on to someone new. The manager keeps earning royalties but they've found another talent to coach. They're now earning from the new band and still collecting from the previous... Same pattern...'

'Where do you even find the talent?'

Steven smiled. 'You don't need talent. You need a story to sell. That's all it is really.'

'Sounds complicated.'

'Well it's different to what we do here, obviously, but it's not that complicated.' Steven shrugged. 'But we aren't here to train you up on my next business venture. We're here to train you up for the job I'm leaving.'

Nate laughed. 'I kind of feel like I want to be trained up on the other one now.'

'I could tell you more but, I'd have to kill you.'

Nate watched as Steven took another swig of his coffee.

Nate asked, 'You know what would make it better?'

'A cheap hooker taking a shit in it would make this taste better but probably not what you're thinking.'

'Biscuits.'

'Looked in the cupboard?'

'They have biscuits here?'

'Sometimes. But, you have to do the snap test first. Another little tip right there.'

'The snap test?'

'Snap it and see if it crunches. If it doesn't crunch, throw that shit away because I promise you, when you bite down on it, it'll be soft.'

'Gross.'

'Yeah.'

Nate got up and walked over to the cupboard. He opened it and a packet of open biscuits fell out from where it had been carelessly placed by whoever had helped themselves the last time. As sod's law would have it, the open packet fell directly into the bin. Worse yet, it landed straight onto the pile of discarded, half-masticated chicken curry someone had tossed out the previous day after failing to finish it on their lunch break.

'Shit.'

Nate looked at the biscuits. There were only a couple left and both had slipped far enough out of the packet to land themselves in the mushed food.

'That's that then.'

'Or it's a chance to play the game for yourself,' Steven said.

'Huh?'

'You can answer the question we'll be asking all day.' Steven nodded towards the biscuits and asked, 'How much to..?'

'What?'

'How much to pick those biscuits up, scoop up some of that sludge and eat it?'

'What? Fuck off. There's not enough money in the world!'

'Really? It's only biscuits and left-overs.'

'From yesterday.'

'Not even a full twenty-four hours.'

Steven reached into his jacket pocket and pulled out his wallet. He set it down on the table before he flicked it open. Nate watched, curious. Steven hooked out a fifty pound note and set it next to the wallet.

'I'll give you fifty pounds to scoop some of that shit up and chow it down.'

'Not happening.'

Steven took another fifty from his wallet.

'You'll give me one hundred pounds?'

'To scoop it up and wolf it down. Got to chew it, got to savour it and got to swallow it. One hundred pounds to eat two biscuits.'

'And you'll really give me the money?'

'Put it in your pocket first, if you want.'

Steven took the notes and handed them to Nate who, in turn, pocketed them.

'But you have to eat them both.'

Nate shrugged. 'Just two biscuits and yesterday's leftovers, right?'

'Right.'

Steven sat back in his chair and watched as Nate picked up the first of the biscuits. He paused a moment and then shovelled up some of the wet debris before standing up straight with it just a few inches from his mouth. The smell hit him in an instant. The curry might have been sitting out for less than twenty-four hours but with the current heatwave and lack of air-conditioning in the building, it stank like a festering, putrid body.

'Rules are,' Steven said, 'once you have agreed your price and taken the money then you can't back out.'

'Really?'

'Those are the rules.' He nodded towards the biscuit. 'Nom nom nom.'

'You think the company will mind if I call in sick tomorrow?'

'They might not pay you for the day but, hey, you got a hundred pounds, right?' Steven smiled. 'They probably won't sack you either.'

Nate wasn't listening. He was staring at the biscuit as some of the gunk started to dribble closer to the edge.

'Don't spill any,' Steven said. 'That wasn't part of the agreement. Now, eat up. It's not getting any fresher.'

Nate closed his eyes and opened his mouth, ready for a bite.

'Wait!' Steven stopped him. 'Kudos for going ahead with it but, we have a long day ahead of us and you need to pay attention. I don't need that fucking your gut up before we get done. But, and this is important... The subjects waiting for us... They don't get a reprieve. If they win the bid, they have to do *everything*. Understand?'

Nate tossed the biscuit into the bin and nodded.

'Good,' Steven continued. 'Then let's get going. We have a busy day ahead of us.'

'I'm keeping the hundred by the way,' Nate said as Steven led the way to the door.

Steven laughed. 'It's counterfeit. You're welcome to it.'

He opened the door and gestured for Nate to lead the way. Nate left the room and Steven followed, keen to get the last day out of the way. The door closed behind them. The left-over curry continued to fester.

The corridor on the other side of the small kitchen was overly long and intimidating to those who didn't know the building. They'd stand at the far end of it and look down it and to all the doors leading away to other rooms. It also didn't help that everything was so brilliant white. The floor was white tiles, the walls were painted white, the ceiling, white and the odd greyscale painting, hanging on the wall, was also framed in white. Along the ceiling there were long strips of light too, which seemed to make everything that little bit brighter still, and even more clinical looking. In the air a strong scent of cheap disinfectant lingered, choking all those who breathed in too deep.

'Cleaners really like their bleach, huh?' Nate couldn't help but to make a comment as the stink started to sting his already dry eyes.

'You get used to the smell of it,' Steven said. 'And, trust me, you'll actually come to be thankful for it too. I'd rather this smell than some of the other odours you might sometimes catch a sniff of.'

'Well that doesn't sound promising. Like?'

Steven stopped leading the way a moment and turned to Nate. He asked, 'Do you have children?'

'No.'

'So you've never been around a new-borns first nappy change?'

'Can't say I have.'

Steven nodded and said, 'Like I said, you'll be thankful for the bleach smells.' He turned and carried on down the long corridor. Nate paused a moment and mulled over what Steven had said. Once it had sunk in, a disconcerted look fell upon his face before he hurried to catch up with his tutor for the day.

At the end of the corridor, Steven turned left. Another long corridor stretched out before them. As Nate caught up he couldn't help but to say, 'This place is like a maze.'

'You get used to it.' Steven added, 'A lot of the doors don't even open.'

'Really?'

'No. I'm just fucking with you. But it makes things easier if you believe it.' Steven explained, 'Anyway I've been here for eight years and I only tend to go into the same rooms time and time again. I suspect I haven't seen more than half of what this building has to offer.'

'You're not curious to look around?'

Steven laughed. 'Maybe I'll ask you the same thing at the end of the day after you see what you'll *actually* be doing here.'

'What do you mean?'

'What did they say about your job exactly?'

'That I'll be interviewing people on a near daily basis. Trying to get into their minds to see what morals people have and what makes them tick.'

Steven shrugged. 'Well they haven't lied to you I guess.'

'You're not filling me with much confidence here.'

'Relax. Like I said, I've been here for eight years now. If it were that shitty, don't you think I would have left long ago?'

'Well, true.'

'And besides, a big part of your day will be spent talking to people and getting to know them and that's the job you said *yes* to so… All good.'

'What about the other part of the day?'

Steven laughed again as he reached *their* door. He said to Nate, 'That's probably something best experienced first hand.' Steven twisted the silver door handle and pulled the door open. 'After you.'

Nate looked into the dark room. Feeling more nervous than he had when he first got to the building for his first shift, he took a step into the room. As he did so, the lights flickered on. Steven stepped in after Nate and only when they were both in did he turn and close the door behind him.

Nate asked, 'Is this it?'

'This is one bit of it.'

The Box

Just as the corridor had been white and clinical looking, so was this room. With the exception of a silver, metal table frame - complete with glass top - in the centre of the room, and two silver chairs, the room was bare. On top of the table, slap bang in the middle of it, there was a cardboard archiving box with the lid still on and locked in place with a plastic tag.

'Are all of the rooms like this?' Nate said, 'Seems like a waste of space. Like, maybe, they could have put this stuff in one of the other rooms with whatever is in those?'

Steven approached the box. He reached into his back pocket and pulled out a flick blade. At the switch of a button, the blade shot out of the top of it, ready to cut away the plastic tag.

Nate walked over to him.

'Take a seat,' Steven said.

'I'm good.'

'Wasn't a choice.' Steven cut the tag away. It fell to the table as he put the blade away and set the knife back in his pocket. He explained, 'We have some reading to do.' Steven pulled the lid off the box and tossed it to the side without a care. He took a seat and looked at Nate with an eyebrow raised, waiting for him to take his own seat. Nate sat.

'So what is this?'

Steven reached into the box and started to pull out beige files. On the front of each of the files, there was a name written in black ink. Capital letters, no less.

'Each of these files is a little bit about the people we're going to be talking to today.' He nodded towards a glass window at the back of the room. Nate followed Steven's gaze.

'What's that?'

When Steven didn't answer, Nate stood up and walked over to take a look for himself. The window looked out into another room. That room, also white, had a number of tables and chairs laid out, much like a classroom.

'That's where we are interviewing them?'

'It is.'

'All the desks. We're talking to them all at once?'

'We are.'

'Isn't it better to do it one at a time?'

'Takes longer. Same questions asked over and over. They won't know how each other answer because they write their answers down.' Steven added, 'This is the best way and, I promise, in the long run you'll be thankful.' He asked, 'Do you know how tiresome it gets going over the same question time and time again? It gets old real fast.'

Nate walked back over to the table and took his seat again. Steven tossed the first of the files down in front of Nate.

'Have a read; get to know our guinea pigs for the day.' He added, 'We have about an hour before they get here and the show begins. Oh and, these are the questions we will be asking.' He reached back into the box and took out a laminated sheet. He put it down on the table in front of Nate.

Nate scanned the sheet and then sat back in his seat, confused. 'What is this?'

'I just told you.'

'This isn't getting to know anyone. This isn't a study. This is just a game.'

'No. It's not. It's a test. How far will someone go to get a bit of money?'

'And the point is?'

Steven smiled. 'The point should be obvious.'

'It should?'

Steven answered, unhelpfully, with a wink.

Nate started looking through the various files, starting at the pictures clipped to the inside of each cover. He couldn't help but notice how each of them looked completely different to the other. Different looks, different ages, different backgrounds.

'These people… They got nothing in common?'

'Nope. All their own people. Individuals in their own right. Pointless having people who are all similar. We won't find what we're really looking for…'

'Which is?'

Steven smiled. 'All in good time. Get reading.' He leaned forward and picked up a file. He flicked to the first page and sat back, making himself comfortable ahead of the heavy reading.

Nate watched him a moment unsure as to whether he was being serious or not. Given the *tests* were supposed to start within the hour, it would have made sense for them to be given the files the previous day, at the very least. It definitely made more sense than giving them an hour of reading time.

Nate couldn't help himself. 'You're being serious?'

Steven stopped scanning his page and looked up to his trainee.

'We really have to read these now? Like, you didn't get to take them home with you the night before? They want us to talk to these people and learn from them but they don't give us much preparation time to at least learn the basics about them first? It doesn't make sense.'

'It makes perfect sense. We have the basics here. We don't have too much time to really dwell on who they are. A quick scan of the basics and then straight in there to talk to them without being too over-familiar with them.'

'Then why let us read anything about them?'

'Well I'll be honest, it's not obligatory. It's just something I like to do because, before we go in, I like to make a wager with the person I'm working with.'

'A wager? On what?'

'On who we think will be the one who wins.'

'Is there anything really to win from this?'

'You mean other than a potentially life-changing amount of money? Yes. There's more to it than that.'

'Like what? I'm sorry but I just don't get all of this.'

'And as I said earlier, you will.' He nodded back to the folders and said, 'Pick one.'

Nate shook his head, confused, and picked the closest file to his left hand. **Svenja Böttle**.

Svenja walked into the office building and approached the long reception desk, blocking the way to the elevators. She joined the short queue and immediately called forward by the dark-haired receptionist the moment they came free.

'Good morning,' the receptionist said with a broad, well-practised smile. 'Who are you here to see?'

Svenja didn't actually know. The letter of invitation just gave a time and a date, with very little else on it other than a warning about leaving plenty of time to park if she was driving in. Svenja handed the letter over to the receptionist who gave it a quick scan before passing it back.

'Ah. Not a problem,' the receptionist said, immediately recognising the invitation; typed up on headed paper. She took a clipboard from close to her keyboard and placed it on the desk in front of Svenja. 'If I can just ask you to sign that please. And, if you came by car, can you please make sure to put your registration number down.'

There was a white biro pen, attached by a chain to a plastic stand on the de. Svenja took the pen and signed her name before adding her licence details. Once done, she returned the pen and handed the clipboard back to the receptionist.

'Perfect. Thank you.' The woman explained, 'Okay you'll be up on the 42nd floor. The elevators are just around the corner to your right . When you get up to floor 42, take a left and there'll be a set of double doors directly in front of you. Just go through those, into a small waiting room, and take a seat. There's already a few of the other candidates up there, waiting.'

'Floor 42,' Svenja confirmed.

'Yes.'

Svenja smiled. 'Thank you.' With that, she turned away from the receptionist and headed for the elevator as the lady on the desk asked the next person to step forward.

Svenja walked away from the receptionist's desk and turned the corner. True enough, the elevators were facing her. As she approached them, a burly looking security guard nodded her a little *hello* as he pressed the call button for the lift. Svenja stood and patiently waited before, to her right, one of the elevators *pinged* its doors open.

'Have a good day,' the security guard said as Svenja stepped into the lift.

The doors closed, sealing her in and, the moment they had, she pressed the corresponding button for Floor 42. Even if the rest of the letter's promises were bullshit, she thought, at least there'd be a nice view.

The elevator jolted violently before it started its ascent up to the forty-second floor. The journey made more "pleasant" with pan-pipe music coming through a speaker in the top corner.

Svenja made the most of the ride by fixing her long dark hair in the wall mirror at the back of the lift. It was a blowy day outside and despite her best efforts at making herself look presentable for this, she looked as though she'd been dragged through a hedge backwards.

Typical.

The elevator jolted again as it came to a sudden stop. The doors pinged and slowly opened with a slight, almost-worrying judder. Svenja stepped out into the clinical looking corridor and turned left, just as the receptionist had instructed. And, just as promised, there were double doors directly in front of her.

'Okay. This is it.'

Despite almost talking herself out of attending the meeting, she took a deep breath and slowly exhaled before she pushed through the double doors and into the waiting room beyond.

The Desperados

The double door to the waiting room swung open and Svenja walked in confidently. Immediately the conversation in the room hushed as Billy Smith, another of the candidates, said, 'Oh look out. Another *Desperado*.'

The room laughed as Svenja looked at him with a puzzled look, unsure as to whether she was meant to be offended by his words, or just confused.

'Don't worry about him,' a middle-aged lady named Michelle Ehrhardt said as Svenja took one of the few remaining seats. She explained, 'It's a nickname he has given all of us, himself included.'

'Oh.'

'Because,' Michelle continued, 'we're all desperate enough for money that we dropped all of our current plans to come to this interview without really knowing much about it.'

'Yeah, no offence intended,' Billy said as he was still chuckling to himself. 'Just a bit of fun.'

Svenja didn't know what to say and just took her seat, along with the other *desperados*.

'You need a name tag,' Michelle said. She pointed to a table in the corner of the room where there were only a couple of name badges left to be collected. Svenja walked over to the table and collected the one with her name printed upon it in bold. Copying the others, she clipped it to the front of her blouse and took her seat once more. She scanned the other names; Michelle Ehrhardt, Trudy Russell, Simone Moriarty, Dean Watts, Jennifer Adams, Audra Walgenbach and - the man who had *joked* when she first entered the room, Billy Smith. She smiled at them all nervously.

'Well what I've learned from this so far is that women are more desperate for money than their male counterparts,' Billy said. Svenja looked at him and raised an eyebrow wondering if this was another of his jokes. 'Where are all the men?'

'Too busy cheating on their wives and girlfriends to attend,' Jennifer said bitterly.

Billy laughed. 'Okay well we now know why you're here seeking extra riches,' he said.

'Oh?'

'Husband has a side-chick on the go and you want out but your shitty little job... Maybe a shelf-stacker? Your shitty little job doesn't quite afford the luxury of being able to just leave him, huh?'

Jennifer went quiet. In fairness to Billy, it was a pretty good guess.

'Although that just blew my theory out of the window,' he muttered to himself.

If only to move away from the awkwardness of Jennifer's situation, Michelle asked, 'Your theory?'

Billy nodded. 'You,' he said as he pointed to Dean. 'Why are you here?'

Dean looked almost embarrassed to be singled out and shifted in his chair uneasily. He was quite happy sitting in the sidelines of this conversation, not wishing to go either side of the fence. He cleared his throat and said, 'Well my house needs a few...'

Billy interrupted him. 'Knew it. Home improvements. Am I right, or am I right?'

'Well, yeah.' Dean shrugged and sat back in his chair, hoping that was to be the last of his involvement.

Billy looked smugly at Michelle and continued, 'I'm here because I had an accident on my bike. Not sure I'll be riding it again any time soon but, if I am, I need a new bike because... Well... I need a new bike. Those things aren't cheap. So, again, practical.'

'I don't see where this is going.'

'Well - guys are more practical than women. So I was sitting here guessing you all wanted more money because you had ramped up your credit card bills, you know? Get the extra cash and get the joint accounts back in good standing before the husbands find out. But then...' Billy peered at Jennifer's name badge and continued, 'Jennifer just blew my theory out of the water with her wanting a divorce.'

'So all women are shopaholics with no ambition or drive other than to go on shopping sprees?' Michelle felt her face start to flush as her blood began to boil.

Billy laughed. 'Just a theory.'

With the most perfect of timing, the door opened and two more attendees walked in. Their names were Steven

Edwards and Laura Hickman. Billy's eyes locked on Steve immediately.

'Here hoping to win the cash for some home improvements?' Billy asked.

Steven looked startled for a second, at having been practically jumped upon by this strange man the moment he walked in, but answered regardless, 'Nope. But it might help to clear some of my gambling debt,' Steven said.

Michelle couldn't help but sit there with a smug look which only seemed to grow the moment Laura added, 'I'm here because I want a swimming pool. That's home improvements, isn't it?'

The other women in the room also couldn't help but to smile as Billy sat back, quiet.

'You need a name tag,' Michelle said as she, once again, pointed to the far table. Michelle was also relieved to see the end of Billy's conversation too. She didn't want to confess to him that, actually, she *was* there because the money would wipe her debt off. She wasn't a shopaholic though, which he would have presumed. She was an adult student and the cost of obtaining her degree was certainly making short work of her low monthly wage. She already knew though that, if any of that had come out in conversation with this idiot, he would never believe that she was trying to further herself with an education. He would have just brushed that under the carpet and mocked her about her spending habits. Michelle glanced over to him. He looked like a dirty Father Christmas. Santa, if Santa had had a problem with eating and drinking. A Santa who hadn't ever washed. In her mind, she couldn't help but wonder how satisfying it would be to punch him square on the nose. She grinned.

Billy noticed her smiling and grinned back, thinking she was just being friendly.

'So,' Steven said as he took his seat, 'you guys are the competition, huh?' With a huge dose of arrogance in his voice, he added, 'Might want to go home now, save yourself the embarrassment because I tell you what - that money is coming home with me.'

'We'll see,' said Jennifer who, up to this point, had been relatively quiet.

Steven looked at her and winked. She was easy on the eye and, although he didn't say as much, he'd gladly give her some of the prize money in exchange for a quick rub down out the back. Jennifer looked away from him.

'So what's your story?' Billy asked Jennifer.

'What makes you think I have one?'

'You wouldn't be here if you didn't need the money.'

'Maybe I just wanted the money. It's a lot of money on offer. I might not necessarily need anything. Could just want the cash in my bank for a rainy day,' she said, not giving anything away.

Billy smiled. 'Ah. So you can go on a shopping spree, huh?'

Jennifer rolled her eyes. 'Yeah, totally.'

Billy said, 'All the same.'

Before he could turn himself into any more of a *public enemy number one* figure, the door at the back of the room opened and Nate Stephenson and Steven Gibson walked in. Under Steven's arm he carried a clipboard. Both men had stern expressions.

'Good morning,' Steven said. 'I'm Mr. Gibson and this is my associate, Mr. Stephenson. We will be conducting the interviews today and, as promised in your welcome letter, awarding *one* of you with the full amount of money.'

Simone asked the burning question, 'I'm sorry but what exactly is the day going to entail? The letter just said we were to be a part of a research program. I tried calling the number provided to learn more but could never get through...'

'I'm sorry. Staff cut-backs and all that. It's not always easy to answer all the calls,' Nate said. Steven looked at him and nodded in approval. It was a good line. His colleague took over from him.

'Rest assured everything will be explained in the next room and...'

'We're not going to have to give blood or anything like that, are we? I'm not very good with needles,' Simone continued.

Steve Gibson sighed and repeated his sentence, 'Everything will be explained in the next room. If you do not like what we have to say, or you feel uncomfortable at any stage - up to the final one that is, then you will be welcome to leave. But, of course, if you choose to go then you walk away with nothing.' He paused a moment, looking from face to face of the volunteers, half-expecting one of them to say something. 'Does anyone have any questions?'

No one spoke but it was obvious that more than one of them had at least one question they wanted to ask.

'Then if you would like to follow us, we shall get the interviews underway.' Steven turned from the room and headed down the corridor beyond the door he'd only just entered from. Nate waited for the group to follow him and then took up the rear to ensure no one got left behind.

The door gently swung shut behind Nate.

The door-lock clicked across, sealing them in.

It's Just A Game

Each of the applicants took the seat, already assigned to them, in the classroom-style room. All of them looked very nervous. None of them had known exactly what to expect from any of this but that didn't mean they were thinking they'd have ended up sitting in a classroom of all places. Just as the hallways had been white and clinical, so was the room. Even the desks the applicants sat at were white, with silver legs. The chairs were also made from a smooth, white plastic.

All of the desks faced forward with Mr. Gibson (Steven) and Mr. Stephenson (Nate) standing at the front. Behind them, there was the two-way mirror which, from this side, just showed a reflection of their backs and the confused faces of the applicants.

'Everyone looks so nervous,' Mr. Stephenson said with a grin. This was all new to him. He hadn't yet seen people put in this position so wasn't used to their reactions yet. To him though, he figured they'd be excited at the prospect of walking away with all the money. But then, maybe that was why they were nervous. Maybe they were so desperate for the cash that the thought of being so close to winning it, only to lose it at the last hurdle, was too much to bear?

Big mouth Billy spoke out, 'So you going to tell us what this is all about then?'

'It's just a little game,' Mr. Gibson said with a smile. It wasn't a smile which brought comfort to anyone though. If anything, he appeared smug. Like he was getting off on the fact he knew something that they didn't.

'Care to elaborate?' Billy found himself getting wound up by these two idiots. How hard was it for them just to be straight with them and say what was going on? For all he knew, he had inadvertently walked into a time-share meeting and they were actually about to try and sell him a load of shit he didn't want, or couldn't afford.

'Maybe they will if you let them speak,' Michelle snapped.

'And maybe you might want to change your tampon before they get going, you moody bitch.'

'Okay,' Mr. Gibson said with his hands raised in front of him. He waved the group quiet and only when all eyes were back to him did he resume. 'Have any of you heard of the game *How Much To..?*' He looked around the group. Most of them were frowning, confused by his question even though it was straight forward enough. But then, other groups who'd been asked the same thing had looked at him with the same expression too. No doubt it was because they weren't expecting to be asked about a kid's game. On the off chance they hadn't heard about the game, he continued, 'Today you will be asked a series of questions. All of them will start with the question *how much to…* Once the question is asked, all you need to do is write a figure down on the form we give you. The figure could be anything you see fit. Your price for completing such a task… For example, how much would you want in order to set fire to a box of puppies?'

'What?' Audra was genuinely shocked by the question. 'I wouldn't answer.'

'Well you have to put *something* down if you want to stay in the game. If you don't want to take part, you are welcome to put your pen down and leave the room though. Once outside, you just need to wait for someone to come collect you and take you out of the building. If you want to stay in the game though, you put a figure down but, again, it can be as high as you want. For example, you could put five million pounds down and your neighbour could put, say, four million pounds down. They would win that round *but* you might still win over all. You see, you will be asked a number of questions and you will put a bid down on the form. At the end of the questions, the forms will be collected up and total amounts added together. Whoever has the smallest figure wins. So, yes, you might say five million to burning a box of little dogs but the rest of your figures could be so small that you still end up winning.'

'So,' Steven said, 'you ask us questions and we put down what we would charge you to complete such a task.'

'Yes.'

'And that's it?'

'In a nutshell.'

Steven asked, 'So how do we win the money?'

'Like I said, whoever has the smallest amount by the end of the questions wins *but* they *have* to go through with all of the tasks asked of them.'

Audra said, 'So even though I lost the puppy question, if I have the least amount when all figures are added together, I would still have to burn them?'

'If you want the money.' He added, 'But don't worry about the puppies. We're not about to be burning any dogs. They're perfectly safe.'

'I should hope not!' Audra was disgusted at the prospect of setting fire to puppies in exchange for cash; it was both inhumane and ridiculous. Even so, she couldn't help but scan her eyes around the room as she wondered whether anyone else *would* have burned that box.

Steven asked a second question, 'So what if we don't win because our rates are too high?'

'Just that. You don't win.'

'Do we get a chance to renegotiate?'

'No, sir. You get to answer the questions once so, for the sake of being crystal clear, you want to go in with the *lowest* amount of money you would accept for completing such a task but you must also keep in mind that if you go through and come out with the lowest amount... To win the money, you *must* complete all of the tasks.'

'This really is stupid,' Billy said.

Steve turned to him, 'Hey, feel free to leave now if you want. To me, this is easy money.'

Svenja was quietly sitting at the back of the classroom. She was concerned with the whole situation. To her, there was no such thing as easy money. Everything came at a cost and if this man's example was to burn a box of puppies, what were the actual questions going be? There was a part of her which wanted to just get up and leave now but, at the same time, she was curious to know how the day was going to pan out. What if the puppies were just an example to make some of them leave immediately and the actual questions were tamer and easier to do? She put a shaking hand up in the air to ask a question.

'Yes?'

'And we can leave at any time?'

'If you're not happy to continue, you may leave at any time. Again, you will just set your pen down and leave the room. You will wait outside and someone will come along and fetch you. That is it.'

'Why us?' Michelle still didn't understand why she had received a letter. What made her so special that she had received an invite compared to, for example, her neighbour?

'Think of it as a lottery system. It's all done based on your National Insurance Number.'

Michelle continued, 'And you say you have done this before?'

'We do it every other month or so.'

'But why?' She pressed for an answer. Whilst she relished the idea of walking away with some much needed money, the whole set-up just seemed off to her.

'Does it matter why? We are offering you money in exchange for a little time and a silly little game.'

'Can leave right now,' Steve said, desperate to push the others out so he could just claim the money as his own.

'No thanks I think I'll stick around and see how it plays out,' she said with a *fuck you* look plastered on her face.

'Any more questions?' Mr. Gibson asked.

No one said anything. He turned to Nate and gave him a nod. Nate, in turn, took the clipboard from his colleague and removed some "answer" sheets from within. He started walking around the classroom handing them out. Each of the applicants looked down at the sheet but there was nothing to see but blank lines onto which they could put their figures down when required to do so. Once the sheets were handed out, Nate went around and handed out some cheap pens. He returned to the front of the room and stood next to Mr. Gibson.

'Thank you, Mr. Stephenson.' He continued, 'Now, this is important, when we start the questions you are *not* to talk to one another. If you discuss your figures, you will be asked to leave and will not be permitted to return. You must come up with your figures on your own but do keep in mind, for the final time, you are bidding the *lowest* amount of money required to complete a task. Is that understood?'

They nodded.

'Good. Now before we start, does anyone need a bathroom break?'

Trudy quickly raised her hand.

'My colleague will show you where…'

'No, no… I just have another question,' Trudy said.

'Oh?'

'How many questions are there in total?'

Mr. Gibson smiled. 'There are ten questions.'

Billy laughed. 'What's the matter? Got to get home to your husband on the off chance he decides to come home to you instead of his side chick?'

'Any other questions?' Mr. Gibson asked before another little argument could break out.

'The letter just said we were going to have the opportunity of getting a life-changing amount of money,' Steve said feverishly, his mind thinking of all the things he could spend it on and how much *more* money he could get once he had gambled some of it. 'How much money are we actually talking?'

'Well that depends on you. Whatever your figure is at the end of the day is how much money you will walk away with, if you complete all the tasks at the end of the day.'

'Then surely we want to put high prices down,' Steve said out loud.

'Well yes, you could think like that. But then you risk pricing yourself out of the game. It all comes down to how greedy your fellow applicants are. If you end up with, say, ten thousand pounds but they end up with five thousand written… You won't get the chance to go and do the tasks. You're out.'

Steve sat back in his chair. This clearly wasn't as straight forward as he had been hoping. Had it not been for a bidding-style way of winning, he would have just put millions down for each answer and been done with it. But what if one of the others wasn't as greedy? What if they were happy with just ten thousand pounds in their back pocket? 'Fuck,' he muttered.

Mr. Gibson laughed. 'See. Not that simple, is it?'

'I still don't understand why though,' Michelle said, more or less to herself. 'It all seems pointless.'

'And, again, you're welcome to leave if you so desire.' He paused a moment and asked again, 'Any other questions or can we get started?' When the room failed to respond to him, he continued, 'Then we shall begin.'

Question One

How much to…

The first question was simple enough. Each of the applicants were asked how much they would charge to drink a pint of cold gravy, left to congeal over the course of twenty-four hours. Not only would it be thick and lumpy but, in the time left to stand, there'd be a thick skin over the top of it. Now a sip wouldn't count as "drinking a pint". The fee they had to put down would be to drink the *entire* pint. If any lumpy bits were left at the bottom of the jug, they'd have to scoop it out with their fingers and chow that down too. Whilst none of the group relished the idea of drinking such a cocktail down, it wasn't *that* bad in the great scheme of things but therein lay the problem. If it wasn't that bad, then surely everyone else would be setting their price low, potentially giving them an early lead to the game which might prove vital as the questions got, undoubtedly, trickier.

Steve laughed as he put his price down within seconds of the question being asked. The moment he finished scribbling it down, he set his pen to the side of the paper and looked around the room confidently. The others all looked as though they were really mulling it over which just made him laugh harder. It didn't matter what they put down, he had won as far as he was concerned. Hard to outbid "free", unless of course you were willing to *pay* to drink it. The smile faded from his face. Was that an option?

He raised his hand.

'I have a question.'

'Sorry. Question time is over.'

He lowered it, like a chastised school boy. He looked around the room for a second time. This time, he wasn't as confident. They never said you couldn't put a negative amount of money down. Surely, if that was against the rules, they would have said. But then, maybe no one else had tried that before? He forced a smile back on his face, trying to put the others off with his now-false confidence. All the time, in his head, he was muttering *fuck*.

The rest of the group hadn't thought the same way as Steve, with regards to offering money to drink the stale mixture. They too were trying to keep their prices low at this particular point although, again, no one had offered to drink it for free like he had, given they didn't know this was an option to give.

As Jennifer wrote down £5, she couldn't help but gag at the thought of winning. If she won, she needed to actually drink this and straight away she could imagine exactly how it would feel, cold and slimy, running down the back of her throat. Before she even realised what she was doing, her face had pulled a *disgusted* look and she had scrunched her nose up. She wasn't the only one feeling queasy about drinking it.

Simone put £50 down on her form. She knew the others would most likely put lower amounts down but she wasn't playing the "game" to beat them. She was thinking, *what is the least amount of money I would want to accept for doing this challenge?* The way she saw it, if she lost she lost. It wasn't as though she had the money anyway so she would be leaving with nothing but the knowledge she hadn't sold herself short. Truth be told she wasn't even sure if she could swallow a pint full of gravy anyway. She liked it with her meats and potatoes, served up hot over a Sunday roast. She had even been known to mop up the gravy juices with bread before but never once had she looked at the left-over gravy jug and been tempted to drink it. She set her pen down. She wouldn't do it for less than £50.

'Not long left to think about it,' Steven Gibson said as he scanned the room to see who hadn't yet put a figure down. As he did so, Nate Stephenson was walking amongst the applicants, looking at their sheets to see what the starting amounts were like. As he glanced down at the pages, he kept a blank expression on his face so as not to give anything away.

The other bids came in as follows:

Laura = £10.00

Dean = £5.00 (written as *a fiver* on his sheet)

Audra = £20.00

Trudy = £25.00

Michelle = £50.00

Billy = free

Svenja = £10.00

After the first question, not that the applicants knew the standing, the results saw Billy and Steven tying for the lead with their bids of drinking the gravy for free.

Steven Gibson scanned the room once more. 'Okay, so everyone should have a figure written down now then?' He glanced to his colleague who stilled walked around the classroom. When Nate saw his look, he nodded back - a non-verbal way of saying they were good to move onto question number two.

Steven Gibson smiled. 'There, that wasn't so hard was it?' He laughed. 'And not a burned puppy in sight,' he said as he looked at Audra giving her a little wink. She didn't respond. He continued, 'Now, with the first question out of the way, is there anyone who wants to just pack it in now and leave? If this isn't for you, there is no shame in walking away now or else you'll just be wasting your day.'

Jennifer showed no emotion but her heart was racing. She really wasn't keen on winning this money if she would *have* to complete all of the tasks, regardless as to whether she won each of the questions with a lower bid but she didn't have anywhere else to go. She couldn't go home; not with him being there, stinking of his other woman. Did he really not realise that her cheap perfume and cigarettes clung to his clothes? Was he really that stupid? Jennifer also knew that if she wanted to be able to break away from him, she needed money and this was for sure the quickest way of getting it. She realised the man asking the questions was staring directly at her as though he could see her unease at being present in this room.

'Like I said, if you want to leave now there is no shame in it. Some people just aren't cut out for this.'

Jennifer forced a smile. 'I'm good.'

'Well, okay then.' He glanced at all the faces. No one looked as though they were ready to get up and leave much to his delight. It always kept things more interesting when people hung on to the end. It certainly made the result readings more exciting if there was a room full of people desperate to win the cash. He smiled. 'Then,' he continued, 'on to question number two and, I warn you now, things are going to be a little more interesting with regards to the questions asked. The first one was just a taster, so to speak.'

Steve couldn't help but smile. He was a gambling man and, to him, he'd already won. The more interesting the question, the more excited he was to continue.

'Bring it on,' he said cockily.

Both interviewers smiled. Why wouldn't they? They knew what was coming.

Question Two

How much to…

'What?' Laura heard the question, just like the others. She was just shocked. Of all the things to ask, this wasn't something any of them had expected. How could they go from gravy to *this*?

'Do you need the question repeated?' It was a one time offer. 'I will repeat it this time but, moving forward, the question will not be asked again and, whether you hear it or not, you will simply have to guess your bid amount. Do you understand?'

Laura snapped, 'I heard the question. Are you serious?'

'The questions are designed to test you.'

'What is the point of all of this?' Laura continued, 'I don't understand what could possibly be learned from these questions. The whole thing is just pointless.'

'And you're welcome to leave at any time but question time was at the start of the day. You have had your chance to ask the questions and that time has now been and gone so, if you don't mind, can we continue and get the questions out of the way? We still have eight more to go, after you have answered this one. That is, if you still want to answer it. Again, the door is right there and you're welcome to use it.'

'I just don't understand what you're getting from asking all of this,' Laura continued.

Steve turned in his seat and half-shouted, 'Just put a bid down. It's not fucking hard, is it? Or, do us a favour, fuck off.'

Neither Steven Gibson nor Nate Stephenson bothered to silence Steve. He had made a fair point, even if there was colourful language used.

What none of the applicants knew at this stage was that they were being filmed. By the end of the day, when those who'd wanted to leave came to go, they would all need to sign a legal document. The paperwork in question not only stopped them from discussing what they went through but also gave permission for the recordings to be used as part of a new game show the company was looking to produce; a pay-per-view channel whereby viewers would get to watch people do fucked up shit.

With the way Steve had spoken to her, Laura suddenly had no problem with answering the question with a hope he had been the lowest bidder in the first round.

How much to spit in the face of the lowest bidder from question one? With Steve in mind, she entered *£0* onto her form and started to imagine what it would be like to suck up some spit from her saliva glands and gob it into his face. *Fuck him*. She wasn't the only person to note that they'd do this for free.

Michelle was the highest bidder on this particular question, closely followed by Simone. Both of whom had issues with spitting into the face of a fellow human. It was a disgusting, and degrading, act and just didn't sit right with them. Both had entered *£50* onto their paperwork. More than that, Michelle had also come close to leaving the room. If this was question number two then she knew it had the potential to get much, much worse from here on in.

The other results were as follows:

Steven = free

Jennifer = £5.00

Laura = free

Dean = £5.00

Audra = £10.00

Trudy = £15.00

Billy = free

Svenja = £10.00

Whilst Svenja, Michelle, Jennifer and Dean had kept the amount the same as question one, the interesting results were in what Audra and Trudy put down. Both women would take *less* money to spit in someone's face over drinking a pint of cold gravy. To them it was easier to spit in someone's face than to experience a moment of grossness for themselves. Looking over their shoulders as they wrote their answers in, Nate wasn't surprised. In this shitty world, it did seem as though people were out more for themselves than for anyone else. Why worry about hurting someone's feelings so long as your own feelings were saved?

'To me this was an easy question,' Steven Gibson said as he waited to make sure they had all put an answer down. 'You won't be seeing these people again so if you have to spit in their face then so what? It's not like they can't just go and wash it off straight away.' He looked at Laura and continued, 'It's interesting that, at this stage, you struggle. Says a lot about you as a person.'

'That I don't want to spit in someone's face like an animal?' Laura looked at him as though he were scum for thinking it would be an easy thing to do, even though she'd just put *free* down on her form thanks to the way she'd been spoken to.

'Not even to win what could be an obscene amount of money?'

Billy looked down at his form. So far he had put zero down for both question one and two and whilst this put him in good standing to win, it didn't exactly put him on a good footing to win a decent amount of money. He glanced around the room, at his rivals, wondering if they'd made the same mistake or whether they were basically agreeing to do everything for free too. In another eight questions, he guessed he'd know but in the meantime, maybe it was better to start putting *something* down as opposed to *nothing*.

'Things are going to get harder from here on in so, again, if you are not comfortable and wish to leave then you may do so now but, to remind you, you leave with nothing.'

The applicants looked around the room at one another. Michelle pushed herself away from her table and momentarily looked as though she were about to stand to dismiss herself. She hesitated a moment and shook her head as the two interviewers looked at her.

'Sure? It's not going to get any easier.'

'And I am free to leave at any time?'

'You are.'

'Then,' she said, 'there's no harm in seeing what the next question is.'

'Indeed there isn't.' Steven asked a different sort of question though before the one they were all waiting for, 'So what is everyone hoping to buy if they get the money? Do you all have big plans?'

'Well she's paying for a divorce,' Billy said as he nodded towards Jennifer. She immediately turned and glared at him.

'Eat shit!'

Steven Gibson laughed. 'Funnily enough, that leads us nicely into the third question and I have a sneaky feeling that we may just lose some of you here…' He looked at his colleague and asked, 'Did you want to read this one out?'

Having only just been watching the proceedings, Nate was keen to get involved. He was, after all, supposed to be being trained up to replace his colleague so it made sense to dip his toe in further, so as to speak. Nate walked to the front of the room and turned to address the applicants. Despite knowing there was nothing to worry about, he still couldn't help but feel nervous as Steven handed him the question sheet.

'In your own time,' Steven said to him.

Nate took the sheet and read out the question without hesitation.

Question Three

How much to…

Everyone sat in silence for a moment. They were all hoping that it was just Nate's sick sense of humour and not the actual question they were supposed to answer. The only problem was, Nate wasn't smiling or laughing. Both men were just staring at them with no expression on their faces and no hint that this was a joke.

Nate pushed them to answer the question, 'Okay, if you would like to put your answers down on the sheet so we can move on. We don't have all day. Well, we do but it would be nice if we could finish up early and get home for an early evening, wouldn't it?'

Steven added, 'Unless of course there are some of you who would like to leave now? Again, that option is always there.'

Dean asked, 'How much are we talking?'

'Well that's for you to say. Three questions in and you have already forgotten how to play the game?'

'No, not how much money. The quantity. How much are we talking? I think that plays a fairly large part in this question, don't you? And I don't think we can really answer the question properly without knowing the quantities.'

Simone looked at him, surprised that Dean was even asking this, and asked, 'Does it really make any fucking difference?'

'Yes, it does!' Dean continued, 'It's one thing to have a bit on the end of your finger and eat that and quite another to turn around and eat a damned tub of it, right?'

'It's shit!' Simone continued to look at him in disbelief.

'And I have a pack of mints in my pocket. People do it in porn films…'

'What kind of fucked up porn are you watching?' Billy laughed.

Dean continued, 'The fact there are videos of people eating crap suggests we aren't going to die from it so, yeah, it's gross… But that's why you put a bigger amount of money down, right?'

Nate pointed out, 'No discussing the amounts.'

Steven whispered to Nate, 'In fairness they shouldn't be discussing anything.' To put an end to it, Steven added, 'Let's say it's a spoonful.'

'A spoonful of shit. And whose is it?'

Simone asked again, 'Really? Does it make a fucking difference? It's shit!'

'I would rather eat my own shit than someone else's turd,' Dean said, taking all of this very seriously.

'It is human,' Nate said.

'Right,' Dean clarified, 'so we are to eat a spoonful of human crap. At least now we know exactly what is required.' He turned to Simone and said, 'Isn't it better to know all of the facts before making a decision.'

She shook her head and said again, 'It's shit! Human shit!'

Dean shrugged. 'I'm married. It's probably better than my wife's cooking.'

Billy laughed from where he was seated whilst his joint-first rival continued to try and put down a sensible amount of money.

This was a tough one, no doubt. It was disgusting to even contemplate eating faeces but Dean was right;

there *were* films of people eating it as part of their sex games so whilst it would be disgusting, it wouldn't kill them. It might just make them sick. So the real question was, *how much to make yourself vomit?*

'No one wanting to leave?' Nate looked surprised.

Most of the group wanted to go but because they could leave at any time, they were all thinking pretty much the same thing; stick it out and see where it goes. Get out of the room by question ten or, depending on how much money they were looking to get, stay and see it through.

Steven whispered to Nate that most people did this. Occasionally you would have someone get up and leave but, for the most part, they'd hang about to see how bad it would get and *then* leave. At least, *some* of them would then leave. By question ten most people were looking at a life-changing amount of money and, when faced with that, they'd do almost anything.

Nate asked the room, 'Has everyone written a figure down yet?'

Compared to the other questions, the monies being asked for had jumped up significantly. The results were:

Jennifer = £15,000

Jennifer figured it would, at least, pay for a divorce.

Laura = £50,000

Dean = £25,000

Simone = £100,000

Audra = £25,000

Trudy = £50,000

Michelle = £10,000

Billy = £1,000

Svenja = £50,000

The only low figure came from Steve who put *£250*. He didn't want to eat crap but he also knew the next questions were going to just keep getting worse. He figured a low amount now would hopefully give him a little breathing space for later questions but *also* keep him firmly in the lead. Besides, with a good hand, he knew he could double his money later.

Michelle said again, 'I just don't understand the point of all of this. Do you get some kind of sick kick from all of this? And what about for the winner when they have to do all of these things... Does that get you off too?' Her rant was ignored.

'We all got our figures in or does anyone need a little more time?'

'Yeah you answer the others but you can't answer me, huh?' Michelle felt her blood start to boil for a second time. She figured it was a simple enough question which deserved an answer but the truth was, she wasn't owed anything. She had been given the choice to leave, or continue. She had been invited here, by letter, and she had *chosen* to come by. The fact they didn't answer her this time was neither here nor there. Yes it would have been nice to have the answer to her question but, really, what difference did it make to her predicament?

Nate looked at her and repeated what his colleague had said earlier, 'You are welcome to leave at any time.'

'I don't understand why you can't answer the question. It's not like I am asking anything untoward, is it? Unless you have something to hide that is?'

'We have nothing to hide and,' he continued, 'by the end of the day, you will have all of your remaining questions answered. Until then, we really do need to go through the questions *we* have mapped out for you.'

Steve couldn't keep quiet and said to her, 'Can we just get on with the questions at hand? If you're not happy with it, please feel free to leave, just as they keep telling you!'

'Shut up,' Michelle snapped back. She was sick and tired of these assholes.

Steve pointed out, 'You heard what they said. We get this done fast, we get to go home! Or, you can just go now.'

'As can you.'

'I don't want to go anywhere. I'm not the one bitching,' Steve said.

'Yeah okay.'

Nate tried to get them back on track and said, 'Okay can we have some quiet please. We really do have to get through these questions and while it is amusing to watch you going at each other, it's not helping with the task at hand. So, let's move on.'

'Yeah… Let's do that,' Steve said as he stared coldly at Michelle who had already turned away from him. With regards to the second question (spitting in the face of the lowest bidder of question one), he couldn't help but hope that *somehow* she had entered a lower amount than the one he had suggested. He would hock up so much shit from his sinuses that he'd issue her a heavy load of green straight into her face with no hesitation. He couldn't help but smile at the thought of doing just that as the fourth question was asked.

Question Four

How much to…

Question four wasn't *that* bad in the great scheme of things. It wasn't the best, mind, because it was definitely going to hurt but Dean, for one, couldn't help thinking that it was easier than having to eat shit. They had to shoot themselves? There was nothing anywhere which said *where* they had to take a bullet, or even what with. For all they knew it was with something small like, maybe, a pellet gun. That was what Dean had convinced himself of anyway and he wasn't the only one to do so. So, to take a shot from a pellet anywhere he chose to administer it… Definitely easier than eating shit.

Dean put his pen to the paper and hesitated a moment before putting in his figure. A little figure in the back of his mind whispered to him, *what if it's not a pellet gun and what if they want you to use a real bullet to a body part of their choice. Sure it's only question four so they still have more to put you through but, what if…?*

Dean raised his hand into the air. Nate looked at him.

Without being offered the chance to go ahead and speak, Dean asked his question regardless, 'What are we shooting ourselves with?'

'Well that you'll find out later, if you win.'

'So we have to blindly put down how much we would want in order to shoot ourselves without knowing *what* we are shooting ourselves with? I mean it's a big difference between shooting yourself with an elastic band and putting a real gun to your body, you know?'

'It's not an elastic band,' Nate said coldly.

'Yet it could still be a pellet gun or even a *NERF* gun. Come on, you gave us a little extra information with the eating of the shit so… How's about a little extra now?'

Nate shook his head. He said, 'Imagine the worst case scenario and put the price down. Or gamble and presume it's not a real bullet and put a different price down. It's entirely up to you. If you knew *how* the games were going to be played at the end of the session then you would answer the questions entirely differently.'

'Well, yeah. If I am to shoot myself with an actual gun I'll probably put a higher sum in. Yes.'

Nate smiled. 'And maybe price yourself out of the market if it's not a real gun.'

Svenja said, 'Real guns aren't legal in this country.'

Nate laughed. 'So what do the armed forces use?'

Michelle spoke up, 'There's no point to this, is there? You literally brought us here to mess with us and see what would happen. There's no way you would ask us to actually shoot ourselves with a real gun. No way. The press would have a field day with *all* of this.'

Nate looked at her with cold eyes and just glared. Steven Gibson was impressed with how Nate was handling the crowd and made a mental note to himself to give him a pat on the back later. Every group was the same; they start off compliant but the further into the game they go, the more they kick up a fuss. If you couldn't control them from the start, you wouldn't stand a chance of getting through the day with the questions being answered. Steven could see Nate would have no troubles once he had left to pursue his other career.

'Just put in the figure you would do it for based on what you *think* is being asked of you,' Nate said firmly. He folded his arms and leaned back on the two-way mirror.

Michelle looked around the room. Was now a good time to leave? The others were already scribbling their figures down. Despite the desire to go, she was curious to see just how far this was going to go. Forgetting that *curiosity killed the cat*, she scribbled a random number down onto the page before her.

As Nate waited for everyone to put their pens down, he said, 'Getting kind of exciting now, huh? And to think, we're only just getting to the halfway mark.'

It was because they were only just getting to question five that, for the fourth time in a row, Steve kept his prices lower than a sane person would. As it stood now, the figures for question four were:

Steve = £100

Jennifer = £10,000

Laura = £15,000

Dean = £500

Simone = £20,000

Audra = £1,000

Trudy = £5,000

Michelle = £20,000

Billy = £500

Svenja = £5,000

The higher figures were put down on the off-chance it was a real bullet they'd be taking. Whilst they could take it anywhere on the body, they would still need to shoot themselves and they would still be in a great amount of pain. And that kind of pain wasn't worth taking peanuts for.

The lower figures were where the applicants firmly believed it was just a trick question and that they wouldn't be shooting themselves with anything which could hurt although, once her pen was down, Audra started to worry that maybe they were meaning for them to shoot themselves in the arm with a needle? She looked down at the lowly sum of £1,000 and started to regret her choice. A grand to become an addict? That wasn't a good trade off.

Audra tried to dismiss the thought from her mind. They wouldn't force them to do drugs. Just as it wasn't legal for the average Joe to own a gun, neither was it legal for them to possess drugs either. It was just her brain playing tricks on her. *But what if it's not? Only a thousand pounds to inject your body with something which can lead to addiction or even kill you?* She glanced up to the door. It was so close and yet seemed so far away. The little voice piped up again, *You can leave at any time.*

Audra wasn't the only person looking at the figures they'd jotted down. Svenja was too. She was confused how her brain had made her hastily jot *£50,000* down to eat a spoon of shit but only *£5,000* down to shoot herself with God only knew what. Apparently her brain was more comfortable with pain than it was at gross things. But then who could blame her? The thought of the festering brown gunk squelching between her teeth as she chewed down on it was enough to make her gag as it was. Let alone how it would actually be when she could taste it.

Audra wasn't alone in her line of thinking; Trudy, Svenja, Billy, Simone, Dean, Laura, Jennifer and even Steven were all more comfortable with being shot than they were at the thought of eating a dollop of crap. In fact only Michelle was charging more to be shot than to eat a spoonful of shit not that they knew what the other person had put down.

'Everyone is so quiet,' Nate said, almost surprised. 'Let us continue… So, how much to shoot *any* other player in the room?'

The group looked amongst themselves and then back to Nate. It would have helped if he had told them *what* they were shooting them with and, again, *where* they were targeting. It was clear from Nate's face that the information wasn't coming though and, once again, they just had to take a guess at what the question could entail.

Steve had no hesitation in putting down *FREE* for the third time but, he wasn't alone. Billy also put down that he would do it for free; even smiling as he did so. The rest of the applicants had also put in low figures - some on par with what they put for spitting in another person's face. By now they had either stopped caring about who was in the room with them or fully believed they'd only be shooting them with something small, such as a pellet gun. They *wouldn't* be asked to shoot them with a real gun, surely.

Nate said, 'Look at you… Hardly any hesitation on that question. In fact, I think that might have been the easiest one! You thought of a number. You didn't argue it or weigh it up. You just wrote that shit down! That's what we like to see!' He laughed. 'Let us continue.'

Question Six

How much to?

If you stripped question six down to the core, it was the equivalent of question one and question three but ranged somewhere between the two on the grotesque scale. It was worse than drinking cold, congealed gravy but not quite as bad as having to eat shit although all three would undoubtedly make a person sick. But, really, a shot of blood? Surely this would have made more sense to be question three? A build up to eating shit as part of question six? That was what was going around Trudy's mind at least and she probably wasn't the only one. Although, that being said, the others were already writing their numbers down. She was just sitting there though, mulling it over in her mind. The one burning question being, whose was the shot of blood? Was it to be her blood? Maybe drained from wherever she had shot herself, suggesting she was going to have to put a bullet in her somewhere? Or was it going to be someone else's blood? If so, was it clean? Did it have any diseases? Would it be fresh? Would it be lumpy with dark clotted bits which she would feel lump their way down the back of her throat? Hard bits of scab to chew upon?

As the various thoughts went through her mind, Trudy felt her stomach twist uncomfortably. Just like the shit and the cold gravy, it wouldn't kill her but she *knew* it would make her violently sick the moment she swallowed it down and, for her, that was a problem. Ever since she was young and had a terrible sickness bug, she had a strong fear of throwing up. It was the worry that she was going to choke to death, unable to grab air between each bout of sickness.

She glanced back to what she had put for the first question. Despite her fears of choking to death on stomach bile, she'd only put it down for *£25*. She surprised herself. Thinking back to having to drink the cold gravy, she wouldn't have accepted that amount had it been a dumb party game. Even so, for the sake of consistency and being fairly sure the others would have been lower than her for nearly everything else anyway, she put her price down and set her pen to the side. When she looked up, she noticed Nate was staring directly at her.

'Really struggled with that one?'

Trudy felt her face flush as all eyes in the room fell upon her as though she were an idiot for taking so long to answer. Without an answer which would potentially make her a laughing stock, she simply shrugged and hoped that Nate would move on to someone else.

'What about everyone else? How did you find that one?'

Steve wasn't listening. He was looking down at his sheet and the figures he had given. Whilst he was confident in that he would win, he was starting to worry that it wasn't going to be worth winning. Not with everything that he would have to do to actually get the money. This was another thing he had said he would do for free meaning so far he was going to drink a pint of gravy, spit on someone, eat shit, get shot, shoot someone and now knock back a shot of claret for just three hundred and fifty pounds. He looked around the room and wondered if anyone else had made the same mistake as him or, at least, tried to earn a little money from all of this. Three-fifty? That wasn't even a decent night at a casino. Just as he had done so before, in the many poker games he had played, he tried to hide his emotions as best as he could. His efforts weren't good enough. Steven Gibson, standing at the front of the room, had clocked him and was grinning to himself. In every experiment they ran like this, there was an idiot such as this guy. The worst was a drug addict who ended up doing everything for a hundred pounds just because he wanted to ensure he could at least get *one* hit. It was funny to the interviewers but tragic for him. A man so desperate for his drug fix that he would literally do anything for a hit. Normally the company went on to offer the winners more than the cash but, in this case, they gave him one final hit to remember and injected him with far too much of the good stuff for him to be able to survive and talk about what he had endured. But his was another story and one that wasn't spoken about outside of the office walls.

The figures for question six stood at:

Steven = free

Jennifer = £1,000

Laura = £5,000

Dean = £500.00

Simone = £10,000

Audra = £5,000

Trudy = £2,000

Michelle = £1,500

Billy = £500.00

Svenja = £500.00

Nate said, 'Okay question number seven. We're getting close to the end and still we haven't lost anyone. I hope you realise that, by the end of this, if you're still here and you win… You *will* have to go through with all of this. There is no backing out once we get to that stage. That is strictly against our rules. So, with that in mind, anyone want to call it a day yet?'

No one moved although, for the briefest of moments, Steve considered it. Was it really worth doing all of this shit for such a feeble amount of money?

'Okay. Next question then.'

'Wait!' The suddenness with which Steve called out was enough to make Melissa jump in her seat. 'I have a question about the leaving procedure.'

Steven Gibson looked at him, surprised to hear this thought was crossing Steve's mind. Of all the people to make it through to the end, he would have put money on him. Nate turned to Steven and asked him if he wanted to field this question.

'You can leave whenever you want but when we get to taking your papers, that is the latest. Right up until that point. You will be asked to sign some legal documents and then you will be escorted from the building.'

'Legal documents? Like what?'

'We'll go through that at the time.'

'No. I think we can go through that now. No one said jack shit about signing anything.' Steve looked around to the other applicants. 'Anyone else know we were to be signing shit?'

The group muttered that they hadn't.

'It's just standard stuff. You know, what happens in this room is private… That kind of thing. I can assure you it is nothing untoward and there's no *really* small print you cannot read. Everyone signs.'

'And if we refuse?'

'Then you get absolutely zero compensation for showing up. It's that simple. You see - what we also didn't say is that we understand you have busy lives. So, with that in mind, we try and look after you. So why you might not go away with the big cash sum you hoped for, if you don't win, you at least leave with something to cover your time and the effort you put into showing up. You sign the paperwork, get a little fee and off you trot. You don't sign. We don't pay up. But, like I said, all of this is explained when you go to leave us. Until then we just try and get through the questions as fast as we can to get us through to the next stage.'

'The next stage?'

'Where the winner completes the tasks and gets their money awarded to them.'

Steve shifted in his seat with a nervous energy. He would have been happier knowing all about the legal documents before he started the whole process. There was something about signing paperwork which made him uneasy; probably due to the trouble he got into with loan sharks once, when he was trying to cover his gambling debt. They offered him money, he signed the paperwork and took it. Next thing, he was moving out of his house - which they took - and moving into a little one bedroom flat.

Steven Gibson continued, 'So just to clarify, you have the right to walk out of here and give up right up until the moment we collect your paperwork. Once we have your figures, that is it. You're here for the duration.' He paused a moment. 'Does everyone understand?'

He took their silence as *we understand.*

'Okay so, question seven,' Nate chimed in.

Question Seven

How much to…

Laura looked down to her non-dominant hand and imagined what it would look like, missing a finger. Just like the others sitting with her, she was wondering whether she would have the option of *which* finger she'd be made to cut off. The question was how much to cut off your own finger with a cleaver so it stood to reason that she would be the one to make the decision on both digit and hand and, if that was the case, the natural choice would be to remove the pinky on her non-dominant hand. But what if they were to dictate which hand and which finger? She would still have to remove it *but* it would be their choice and, if so, they probably wouldn't give a shit to hear her opinion on it. Not that it mattered really. Looking at her figures, she knew she wasn't going to be even close to winning the money and having to do any of this. But, like the others sitting in the room, she still couldn't help but to wonder which would be her choice.

Another thought rushed through her mind: What if the cleaver wasn't sharp enough to remove the finger, and bone, in one blow? She'd have to rain blow upon blow down on her hand until the finger separated from the rest of her body. It would hurt bad enough with one quick chop but multiple cuts? She noted that they made no mention of first aid either. The question was straight forward enough: how much to cut the finger off?

More questions: Would she be allowed to pack it in ice and have it ready for a medical team to try and re-attach it? Would she forever be without the finger? Can they even put a finger back on and have it work as it once had or once it was off, would it be useless? Maybe they could put it back on but maybe it wouldn't move like it used to? Was there a time-limit to get to the doctors? She presumed they would be completing all the tasks from the ten questions before such medical procedures would be offered, or at least sought. If so - what were the next questions and how long would they take to complete?

Laura glanced up at the two men standing before the group and tried to read their expressions but, neither man gave anything away. As subtly as she could, she glanced around the room at the others. With the question having only just been asked, they too looked as though they were in deep thought as they tried to figure out what the cost of a finger would be.

She looked down at her own sheet and wondered why she was giving it as much thought as she was. So far she was asking for over *£70,000* to go ahead and do these tasks and she knew that wouldn't be the cheapest option on the table. But therein lay the problem. She didn't know what else was coming. The others might be cheaper up to this point but that didn't mean they would see it through to the end. If they left, leaving her, she would be the winner and despite not relishing the idea of having to do any of this shit, seventy grand was a lot of money. Laura had come here wanting a swimming pool for her home but, this kind of money was potentially enough to put towards a new home which *came* with a pool. And this was only the seventh question. There were still three more questions to come meaning that figure was only going to increase.

She looked back through what was being asked of her: drink gravy, spit on someone, eat a spoon of shit, shoot herself, shoot one of the others, drink a shot of blood and cut her finger off. Seventy grand. That was a lot of money and, quick maths in her head, that would take about three years (or more) to earn on her current wage... With this all going through her head, she kept her next figure low on the off-chance the others did bail out at the last hurdle. Seventy thousand pounds...

As she scribbled down her answer to the question, her mind had already switched over to what she would be spending the money on as soon as she recovered from all of the tasks. She could see the smile on her face, clear as day, when she'd be spending it too. To her, the pain was worth it.

With her figure down, she set her pen down on the table. The moment she did, Nate took a step forward and said, 'Okay, everyone got their figure down? Then the next question... How much to now eat that finger?'

Laura looked at him with shock. So much for looking to get the finger surgically attached once more. Unless, of course, she could swallow it whole and shit it out and then bag it and ice it? She laughed in her head at how stupid that was and - a split second later - once again found herself with a number of questions racing through her mind.

Would the finger be cooked? Would she have to cook it herself? Would it come with a little side salad? Would she have to eat it raw? The thoughts stopped just as promptly as they had first raced to mind. Did it really matter how it was prepared? They were asking her to eat her finger.

To.

Fucking.

Eat.

Her.

Finger.

Steve looked at his sheet. With these two questions the amount of money he could win was starting to look a little healthier. £5,000 to remove his finger and another

£5,000 to eat it. He looked around the room and had a feeling he wouldn't have been the cheapest on this particular set of questions but, being the cheapest on the *other* questions would put him in good standing to win overall though. At least he hoped. In the great scheme of things though, it still wasn't a lot of money to do all that would have been asked of him. And losing a finger? Could make holding a deck of cards a little more challenging? He set his pen down and leaned back in his chair. The back of the chair creaked.

He asked, 'What the fuck are we doing?'

His voice echoed around the room. All eyes turned to him, including those of the interviewers.

Steve continued, 'Seriously? Eat shit. Lose a digit, eat the fucking thing, spit on one another, shoot someone, shoot ourselves, drink a shot of blood… What in the *actual* fuck are we doing?'

'You're only just asking this?' Michelle turned back to her own paper and looked down at the figures she'd been putting in. She had been asking the very same question from the moment the questions started and she saw how dark, and weird, it all was. She kept telling herself that it was just a joke or a way of giving rid of the people who weren't serious about wanting to win money. She couldn't see how any company, no matter who they were, could get someone to do all of this crap. Surely it wasn't legal? But then, why wouldn't it be? They weren't forcing them to stay. They weren't forcing them to answer the questions. If anything, they were going out of their way to remind them - over and over - that they could leave at any given moment should they choose to. Choice. That's what it came down to; choice. It was the choice of the person answering the question how much they could win *and* whether they actually stayed to play the stupid game. But was this all there really was? Or was there something more to it?

Michelle set her eyes on the interviewers. They looked like normal businessmen, standing there dressed in their nice suits with their white shirts pressed. If you saw them out and about, you might even think they were from some financial office somewhere. You certainly wouldn't imagine them running these scenarios.

'I think I want to stop,' Steve was saying.

'Just two questions away from the end. Are you sure about that?' Nate walked over to the door and held it open. 'If so, this is the door you want.'

'It's bullshit. This whole thing is fucking bullshit.'

Svenja agreed with him. Her own figures had been relatively high. Her current total stood at just under £100,000 and whilst that sum of money was one hell of a temptation - this wasn't in her nature. She had come with no money. She was just as happy to leave with no money. Or, more importantly, leave with all her digits intact and fresh breath.

Nate told her, 'And same to you too. If you wish to leave… You are more than welcome to do so.'

Svenja turned to look at Steve, as though she were taking her cue from him.

'Or you could wait around and see what the next question is,' Nate said.

She shook her head. 'I don't think it makes a difference at this point. I don't want to do any of what you're asking us to do so why stay? It's just a waste of my day. They say time is precious and here I am, wasting mine by playing along with this stupid game and for what? I have no intention of hanging around and I know for a fact that I won't be the cheapest person given what I've put as my *fee* in my answers.'

'The next questions might really appeal to you though,' Nate told her, 'and you could claw back the difference from what you've charged to what someone else has asked for, don't you think?'

Svenja laughed. 'I really can't see how any of the questions you ask are going to appeal to me and I don't really understand why you're trying to talk me out of leaving when you said about wanting to get home faster. Surely if you're serious about getting home, you'd just let me go?'

Nate gestured towards the door and said, 'Fair enough. There's the door. Please leave your answer sheet on the table. Wait in the corridor and someone will come and collect you. There'll be a little paperwork to sign but then you're free to leave.'

Svenja stood up and removed her jacket from the back of the seat she'd been sitting on. 'Thank you,' she said as she left the room.

'Yeah, fuck this,' Steve said. The money would have been good but he didn't sign up to lose a finger. Not when it could impact the way he played cards. There'd be other ways to make money.

'Please leave your answer sheet on the table,' Nate said again.

Steve held the pen up and said, 'Fine but I'm having this.' He put the pen in his pocket and followed Svenja out into the corridor as Nate turned to the rest of the room.

'Anyone else?'

Michelle got up and, without a word, left the room. Nate eyed the remaining *contestants*. No one else moved.

'Well,' he said, 'that should make things faster... So... Question number nine, I do believe.'

Question Nine

How much to…

Simone was crying. She knew her figures were high but she needed the money. The youngest of the group, she could set herself up for life if she played her cards right but now her mind was torn. She didn't want to do any of what was asked but at the same time, she *could* set herself up. The student loan - gone. A deposit on a house; a house of her own and not some overpriced shit-hole she'd be throwing money away by renting. Maybe even a car too… Like some of the others sitting with her, her mind had got carried away with spending the cash in her head in-between the questions and she'd run away with the fantasy of the potential life she *could* have lived had she been more realistic with her sums. Realistic? What part of this was realistic? Her mind raced. Like Michelle, Steve, Svenja - and God only knew who else - she knew *none* of this was realistic. This was all stupid and now *she* was stupid. Crying?

What for? Was she crying because she had pissed away the chance of winning money? Was she crying because her brain kept picturing her completing the required tasks?

She put her hand up.

'Yes?' Steven Gibson looked at her and quickly reminded her, 'The question won't be repeated. You'll just have to make your best guess.'

'No,' she said.

'No?'

'May I please use the bathroom?'

Whilst she did need to use the bathroom, her request was also a way of getting away from the madness of the room. If only for a little while. A little break.

'Or we can play an extra little game.'

'What?'

'Right here, right now.'

'Please, I just want to use the bathroom.'

Steven reached into his pocket and pulled out his wallet. Even at just a glance you could see that it was bulging with cash. He walked over to Simone's table and set the wallet down in front of her.

He asked, 'How much to sit there and piss your pants?'

'What?'

'Oh man, just let her use the bathroom,' Dean said.

Steven flashed Dean a glare which shut him up immediately. He turned back to Simone.

'Why are you doing this?' Simone asked.

'What are you talking about? I'm giving you the chance to earn a little more money and all you have to do is piss your pants. How'd you get here? Car? A lift? Public transport?'

'Car.'

'You drove yourself?'

'Yes.'

'So really all you're doing is wetting yourself in front of these people who you'll never see again, yeah? Then - when you go - you're going straight to your car. You park in the car park?'

'Yes.'

'So - what - a ten minute walk? Wrap your jacket around your waist so no one else can see. Walk to the car, climb in, drive home, change. You whittle it all down and, really, it's not that bad.' Steven looked around the room. 'Would anyone else do this? Not an offer. The offer is for this young lady here. But, I'm curious, what would everyone else say if the offer was made to you?'

'Just let her use the bathroom,' Laura said.

Simone ignored Laura and said, '£200.'

Steven looked at her. '£200?'

'To wet myself.' Simone's face was flushed with embarrassment but Steven was right. By the time you broke the question down and looked at what it would actually mean, it wasn't *that* bad. Certainly not for easy money at least.

Steven picked his wallet up and started to count out the notes. 'Ten, twenty, thirty, fifty, seventy, eighty, one hundred…' He set them down in front of Simone and counted out the remaining hundred which he also placed in front of her. 'There you go. Two hundred pounds.'

She looked at him with tears still in her eyes.

'What are you waiting for? You need the bathroom so… Go.'

There was a delay as she tried to relax enough to urinate.

'Would it help if I turned my back? Would it help if we all turned our backs?'

'This is sick,' Trudy said.

'No one asked you,' Steven warned her.

Even Nate was surprised by Steven's actions. He wanted to ask him if this was normal procedure or whether it was because it was his last day. A little bit of fun before leaving for greener pastures. For the sake of professionalism, he kept quiet.

'Do be quick,' Steven continued, 'we still have the questions to get through.'

At first only a dribble of urine trickled from Simone as, once it started, she clenched to stop from pissing herself upon instinct. With the flow started though, it was easier to relax the second time and soon enough, she was relieving herself into her panties. The warmth spread beneath her cheeks and inner thighs as Steven watched her face intently. A tear trickled down her cheek - partly from where she'd been crying earlier and partly from the fresh embarrassment she faced.

Steven's words played through her mind as if to ease her embarrassment, *You never have to see these people again.*

Steven winked at her. 'I have another question,' he said when she'd finished urinating. 'How much to remove those soaked little panties and give them to me?'

'Fuck you,' Simone said, finding her voice.

'You've just pissed yourself for two hundred quid and, what, you're not prepared to make a little more money by giving your knickers to me? You think you'll miss them if you take them off? Just reaching up under your skirt and pulling them down that much of a hardship? To me, it's easy money.'

Billy piped up. 'Well if we're talking easy money, I need a shit if you want to buy that from me?'

No one laughed as Steven turned to Billy with a look of hate in his eyes.

'The fuck you looking at?' Billy wasn't the type of person to sit around getting eyeballed from people he deemed beneath him. He was part of a large biker outfit and if someone came looking for trouble, he was more than happy to give it to them. If they were more than he could handle, then his club associates were always there to have his back. This little prick, in his shitty little suit, wouldn't be a problem though - even with Billy's leg still fucked from when he crashed his motorbike.

Steven turned back to Simone and said, 'Last chance...'

'£500.'

'£500 to buy your dirty panties? Isn't that a little excessive? You charged less to publicly embarrass yourself. Interesting.'

'You asked how much. That's how much.'

Steven reached into the inside pocket of his jacket and pulled out a roll of notes. He set them down on Simone's table.

'Count it,' he told her. 'But I promise you, it's five hundred exactly.'

Simone looked at him for a moment unsure as to whether he was joking. He wasn't. She took the money and counted it out onto the table as the rest of the room watched in silence.

'All there?' He asked when she finally finished.

'Yes.'

'So…' He pointed to her crotch. 'I'll be taking those then.'

'You want me to take them off here?'

'A deal is a deal. You asked for five hundred. I gave you five hundred.'

'Please can I just go to the bathroom and…'

'So remove them.'

Simone hesitated a moment and then stood up. Beneath where she was sitting, there was a small puddle of yellow on the seat of her chair. She unstuck the back of her skirt from her legs and then reached up to her knickers with her shaking hands. She snaked her hips from side to side, and then jiggled her legs until her soaked underwear hit the floor. Steven licked his lips as she stepped back, out of them. Without a word, her face still burning red, she leaned down and picked them up off the floor and handed them to him. He took them from her still-shaking hands. With his eyes locked to hers, he brought the panties up to his face and inhaled deeply before letting out a long sigh.

'You need to drink more water,' he said. 'Sit back down.'

Without arguing, Simone sat back down into her puddle. She was embarrassed and close to more tears but also seven hundred pounds better off.

Seeing the depths of depravity Steven was happy to sink to with Simone was enough for Trudy and Audra though. Both women stood up and walked towards the door which, to his credit, Nate opened for them. If they were happy enough to embarrass this poor girl like that then neither one of them wanted to know how far they could go exactly. There wasn't enough money in the world to be so humiliated and this little stunt just brought all the previous questions and scenarios crashing home to roost.

'Dropping like flies.' Steven laughed.

Nate closed the door and turned back to the room. With a solemn expression on his face he said, 'Does everyone have a figure written down for question number nine then?'

How much to fuck (/ be fucked by) a filthy homeless man?

Simone quickly scribbled an answer down.

'Then, if everyone is done, we shall move on to the final question,' Nate said with a surprising amount of excitement in his tone. 'Nearly there, kids.'

Question Ten

How much to…

The last question and the last chance to bail out. Billy stood up and walked to the door. Nate didn't bother to open it for him. It didn't stop Billy from leaving. He opened the door and stepped out into the corridor where he noticed the others still waiting around for someone to come and collect them. He left the door open so Nate closed it.

'Do we even want to know the last questions?' Michelle looked at him, still morbidly curious.

'Not really.'

'Probably not,' she admitted. 'Even so…'

Billy said, 'How much to let a homeless man fuck you or, fuck a homeless man. I guess the guys have to fuck the man and the women have to be fucked by him.'

'A homeless man?'

'A filthy one no less.'

'So the last question?'

'You have to eat the ejaculate back out.'

'What the fuck,' Michelle turned her nose up at the thought of it and not just because it was a homeless man. She was a married woman. There was no way she was going to cheat on her husband just to get some money. As for eating her semen, it wasn't something she liked to do with him, let alone a stranger. 'I wish I knew what the point of all this was,' she continued.

Billy shrugged. 'I ain't fucking no man and I don't give a fuck what the point of it is.' He looked up and down the corridor. 'We meant to just wait here?'

'That's what they said.'

Back in the room and the figures had been noted. Dean's face was still twisted as he couldn't help but to imagine eating his own spunk back out of wherever he had shot it. It was bad enough the one time he pleasured himself and accidentally got himself in the mouth with it. That split second decision as to whether he needed to spit or swallow. He just hoped that, if he won, he got to say where he shot his load. It would be far easier to eat it out of a rubber or lick it off some guy's chest, even if it was filthy from however-long of living on the streets.

'You don't look happy,' Nate said to him.

'Not exactly my meal of choice,' Dean said sarcastically. 'But then, I guess it will wash the blood and shit down nicely, huh?'

'Something like that,' Nate said.

Steven took charge of the room. 'Okay that's the questions answered. Well done for seeing it through. We will now collect the papers up and see who has won the chance to get the money.'

'Winning?' Laura laughed. 'Is that what this would be called? I don't think anyone could consider it as winning.'

'I'm sure they will when they're out spending the money,' Nate interjected.

'Last chance to leave,' Steven said to the four remaining applicants. 'Once we have the papers, that's it. The winner will *have* to complete all that is asked of them.'

Jennifer, Laura, Dean and Simone all sat nervously, quickly weighing up the options before them. They knew what was being asked was borderline insane but, they also knew the amount of money they had bid down and even though it wouldn't make them a millionaire, it was life changing.

Simone in-particular had a harder time in leaving as she had the seven hundred pounds still on the table before her. That in itself was enough incentive to stay, just because she could envision what the rest of the money would look like, stacked up with this little bundle. It wasn't greed though. It was desperation for a better life and whilst it wouldn't have been easy to do any of the tasks, it was still easier than working however many years it would take to earn the equivalent.

Meanwhile Jennifer was thinking about starting her new life. Her own quick mental add-on brought her sum to around the seventy thousand pound mark. More than enough to get away from her cheating husband and put a deposit down on a place of her own. So many of her friends, also divorced, forced to live on the breadline due to it being hard for them to support themselves with their part-time jobs and children. She didn't want to be like them, not that she had kids of her own thankfully.

The breakup would be hard enough without having children thrown into the mix too.

'Okay then,' Steven said.

Nate walked around the room and collected all of the sheets up. He put them on top of his clipboard and walked back over to his colleague.

'We are going to pop into the other room and go through the sheets,' Steven told everyone. 'Once we are done, we will come back and announce the winner, along with what will happen next. The process shouldn't take that long so, say, give us ten minutes to talk amongst yourselves.'

Without giving them a chance to ask anything, or stall him further, Steve and Nate left the room. The door closed behind them.

Dean asked, 'Anyone else nervous about winning?'

It wasn't a joke yet, when he asked, he still couldn't help but to laugh. Nervous laughter?

Laura said, 'What was it that guy called us? Desperados?'

'The Four Desperados. Sounds like it could be a film.'

Jennifer turned to Simone and asked her, 'Are you okay?' The stench of piss lingered in the air and was hard to ignore. Harder still for Simone to ignore as the drying urine irritated her skin. Even so, she didn't want to talk about it.

'I'm fine.'

Jennifer knew what *I'm fine* meant. She had said it herself on so many different occasions when her own friends had asked after her. Even on her darker days the answer would always be the same. I'm fine. She tried to change the subject and make the traumatised looking girl smile.

'At least you have seven hundred pounds.'

'Yep.'

'What are you going to spend it on?'

There was a slight pause before Simone said, 'Underwear.'

Jennifer wasn't sure if it was a joke or not but couldn't help but to laugh.

'You know you can buy soiled panties online for about fifty quid. You got a good deal out of him,' Dean said in a very matter of fact tone.

'I hope he chokes on them.'

'Yeah. That would be good,' Dean agreed.

'So how did everyone else price up their answers?' Laura asked.

'I can't even remember,' Jennifer said. She wasn't lying. The whole thing was just a blur to her now as her mind focused more on having to actually *do* what had been asked. Could she really go through with it? And what if she refused? She just left without the money? That didn't seem like a bad deal although she knew it would be a decision she'd regret further down the line. *If only you ate that shit. You've eaten enough of it in your marriage. A spoonful should have been simple.*

'We'll find out soon enough,' Dean said.

True enough, in the next room beyond the two way mirror, the numbers had been added together and the winner was clear.

.

Victorious

'Are you surprised?' Steven looked at Nate who was still staring at the page onto which they'd written the results.

'I'm not sure. Should I be?'

'You didn't have a clear winner picked out in your head before they started answering the questions? I do every time I do this. My surprise this time was that Steve guy. He seemed so cock-sure and arrogant, I would have thought he'd have won and looking at his sheet, I was right. Had he stayed he would have but... Well... He's out and this is what we're left with.'

'I guess if I am surprised by anything it's how low the answers are.'

'You would have put higher prices down had you been playing along?'

'Pretty much for most of them, yes.'

'Reckon you would have made it through to the end?'

'Depends how desperate I was, I guess.'

'And that's what drives these people; desperation. Had we called them in one at a time and gone through it, the answers would have been higher. Past experience has taught us that. They're only *low* now because they knew they were in competition with one another. The pressure of out-doing the people sitting with them forced their hand to write down a figure which they wouldn't usually even consider.'

'Even so…'

'Yeah… I'll be honest, I was expecting higher too. Still,' Steven continued, 'could well be a cheap day, hey.'

'I'll say.'

Nate looked back down at the sheet.

Jennifer = £71,015

Laura = £125,060

Dean = £291,010

Simone = £200,150

Steven asked, 'You think she will go through with it?'

His colleague shrugged.

'Not that she has a choice, mind you.'

'What happens if they do say no?'

'It's not an option. One way or the other they have to complete the tasks. That's the rules.'

'Ever had anyone fail?'

'A few people have needed a helping hand.'

'Isn't that cheating?'

'Which is why we deduct £10,000 from the fund for every time they need someone to help them out. When they see their funds going down, it's amazing how many go ahead and push through for themselves. After all, would you rather walk away with all the money and do the tasks or do the tasks and walk away with next to nothing?'

Nate was looking at Jennifer's individual sheet now. Taking the *spit* and *gravy* out of the equation, her third cheapest fee was to drink a shot of blood. The very thought of such a task repulsed Nate and made him feel queasy. It was bad enough sucking on a small cut and tasting the fresh blood but, this? Weirdly Jennifer wasn't the only one to put a low amount down for that particular question. Steve had put down that he would do it for free and a few of the others had said they'd do it for only five hundred; the same amount Simone had sold her pissed-in panties for.

'I just honestly thought the figures would be higher for some of this,' said Nate.

Steven laughed. 'Like I said, desperation and competition drives people to do stupid things. Anyway it's better for the company if the figures are lower. The less we give away to the contestants, the more we raise from the Pay-Per-View. Not forgetting our bonus at the end of the year of course.'

Nate's mind flashed to the talk of wages in his initial interview. There was certainly a lot of money to be made here, so long as you kept the show running and people at home interested in tuning in to see how fucked-up things could get. He couldn't help but to bring up Steven's own departure, 'And you really want to leave this gig behind?'

'I've seen enough.' Steven laughed again. 'Time to move onto new ventures and, besides, there's better money to be made there with the right business mind. Anyway - you want to tell them the results?'

Nate got up from his seat. He shuffled the papers together and nodded.

'Then lead the way,' Steven said. 'Let's get this show on the road.'

My Name Is Jennifer

1.

My heart skipped a beat when the door opened and the two men walked back in. One of them, I forget his name, had the clipboard still tucked under his arm. They stopped in front of us and looked at us for a moment with no expressions on their faces. They gave nothing away as to who could have won.

Won?

Again, was there any winning when it came down to this game? Although, strangely, there was a part of me which hoped they were going to call my name out because I'd already let my mind get carried away with dreams of finally leaving my husband and setting up by myself. Start my life again and hopefully find a man who is worth my time. I deserve better and - as sick as this game was - this was a way to find *better*.

There was another part of me, albeit quieter, which hoped I didn't win though. I'd get to go home and they mentioned some sort of compensation anyway, so long as I signed their papers. It might not be enough to leave Andrew but it would hopefully be enough to treat myself to a nice meal out, or something. Something for me and only me.

My mind went back to that money though. It was a lot of money and I was practically salivating at the thoughts of all I could do with it.

'We have added up the figures,' the guy with the clipboard said, 'and there is a clear winner from those of you who remain.'

I glanced around to the others. They looked as nervous as I felt. I wondered if their hearts raced as fast too.

'In no particular order. Simone, please stand up.'

The girl to my right stood.

'We're going to have to ask you to wait outside with the others. You were not the winner.'

I'm not sure if a wave of relief washed over her, or regret. She collected her seven hundred pounds and walked to the door. She stopped momentarily and turned back to the men at the front of the class. She looked as though she was going to say something. I'm not sure what though. No words came. She turned and left the room, leaving the door open.

'Dean, please stand.'

Dean stood.

'You're out.'

'Fuck!'

The way he swore... Was he really *that* upset? At least he could go without having to do any of the nasty shit they'd asked. Oh God. *Shit*. I can almost taste it now.

'Then there were two,' the man with the clipboard said.

My heart beat harder and I felt sick to the stomach as I looked down to my hands on the table before me. My eyes fixed on my fingers and I found myself wondering which I would choose to lose.

'Can you both stand.'

The woman next to me stood first. She looked much calmer than I felt at this stage. I could even feel the sweat starting to cascade down my back. I stood and tried to ignore my jelly-legs.

'Well we could only have one winner. Laura, your figure was just over £120,000.'

My heart skipped a beat as I already knew what that meant. Worse though, I knew I had under-charged. I could have walked away with another £49,000 and still been the winner. I had sold myself way too short.

'Jennifer…'

I blurted out, 'I'm not sure I can do this.'

My eyes started to well up and my sight started to get cloudy as a result of the tears. Little dots appeared in my vision and I had to take my seat before I fell over.

'Your figure was just over £70,000…'

I looked at the other woman. She was looking at me with an expression of both shock and pity. Maybe a little envy? She'd lost the chance of getting the money but she pitied me because she knew I had to do the tasks. The shock, I presumed, was because there was *such* a difference between our figures.

'… Making you the winner.' He said to the other woman, 'You can leave the room and wait with the others.'

She was still looking at me when she said, 'I'm sorry.' With that, she walked from the room leaving me with the two men.

I said again, 'I'm not sure I can do this.'

'You knew the rules. No backing out now.'

'But I genuinely don't think I can do this.'

'Then you should have left.'

Shaking, I watched as he pulled a chair from one of the other tables. He turned it towards where I was sitting and took a seat. He leaned forward.

'Here is what is going to happen: You will go into the other room. It has been prepared with most of what you need to do already. So, there's a table in there with little bits and pieces of what you need to do. For anything you can't do, or think you can't do... Someone will be on hand to do it for you, but *to* you. Can't cut your finger off? They'll remove it for you. But,' he raised his finger to me as though making an important point, 'every time someone has to do it for you, you automatically lose £10,000 of the money you *could* win. There are ten questions. If you fail to do any of them, you will actually end up owing *us* money, such was the low amount you were charging. Don't do seven of the tasks and you'll walk away with about a grand in cash. Do them all though, you walk away with everything you wanted. It's not rocket science.'

I felt sick. I wanted to run from the room, down the corridor and back towards the elevator which brought us up here. I wanted to but I didn't move. I was rooted to the spot. I don't know why. Fear?

He was still talking, 'I don't know about you but I would sooner walk away with as much money as I can, especially if you're going to be put through the tasks anyway... Just in case you're thinking you can skip a few and just lose ten grand per skipped item... Make no mistake, we *will* be forcing you to do everything.'

He looked at me and raised an eyebrow.

'You understand me?'

I looked directly at him but didn't respond. Everything was a blur and his voice sounded distant.

'Do you understand me?'

I nodded.

'Then let us go through to the other room and start the proceedings. Faster we start, the sooner it is all over.

Okay?' He was looking at me like he wanted a response so, again, I just nodded.

'Let's go,' he said to his colleague before he walked to the door. The second man took me by the arm with a firm grip and marched me from the room. My heart was beating so hard it felt like my whole throat was pulsing. Meanwhile a sickness continued to bubble away in the pit of my belly.

I hated my husband. From the moment I knew he was cheating on me with the office bimbo; I hated him. But right now, I wished he was here with me.

2.

The others were still waiting around in the corridor. They were all looking at me and looked as though they felt sorry for me.

'Please help me,' I begged them.

They didn't say anything or even look as though they were about to step in and stop this though. No doubt they were standing there thinking that I had known the rules of the game and what I was letting myself in for. And they would be right if they were thinking it. I had known. I had just never expected to win and find myself in this position. I had meant to leave. I had meant to leave the room! I got confused?

'Please...'

The first guy stopped in his tracks and backed up until he was standing with the rest of the group. He turned to me. 'Do you know who gave the cheapest price for the first question; how much to drink a pint of gravy?'

He was staring directly at me so I knew the question was aimed at me. I shook my head. How could I know?

'Let me tell you. It was Billy and Steven,' he informed me. He smiled. 'Remember question two? How much to spit in the face of the person who gave the lowest price for question one? Now in fairness the question was in the singular. You have to spit in the face of *one* person so… Being fair… Pick one.'

'What?'

'We're starting with question two first. Choose Billy or the other one.'

'What?'

'Choose one of them. Spit in their face.'

My heart skipped a beat. I looked at all the faces staring back at me. Horror in their eyes which, I presumed, mirrored my own.

'I don't want to do this,' I said.

'It's fine. Spit in my face,' Billy said.

'No. I won't do it.'

'It's *fine*,' he said again.

'No!' I said again, 'I won't do this!'

The man with the clipboard shrugged. He walked over to Billy and handed him a small bundle of fifty pound notes, all bound together with an elastic band. I don't know how much was there.

'What's this?'

The man smiled. 'Compensation.'

'For what?'

'Open your mouth.'

'What the fuck for?'

'Unless you don't want that money. It's a grand, by the way.'

'I want to know what I have to do for it,' Billy said.

'I told you. Open your fucking mouth.'

I watched, nervous, as Billy opened his mouth.

'Wider,' the man with the clipboard said.

Billy opened his mouth wider; a frown on his face.

The man suddenly hocked up a lungful of green into his mouth. A disgusting sound of snot and saliva being sucked into the mouth from both the gut and the sinuses. I could almost hear it bubbling. He turned to the rest of us and opened his mouth. It was almost luminous as he rolled it around, like a gum-ball of mozzarella cheese, half-melted. With a glint in his eye, he turned to a worried looking Billy and spat it directly into his mouth.

Billy gagged immediately when he felt the weight of the phlegm ball land heavy on his tongue. I could only imagine the saltiness of it on his taste buds and I too gagged violently. I closed my eyes as I heard someone else gag too; a worry that someone was going to vomit up their breakfast.

'Swallow it,' the man said.

I couldn't watch but I could hear it as Billy gulped down. A thick wad of cold custard sliding down the back of his throat. The way of was swallowed... It sounded as though the slimy mixture had been lumpy and I could almost hear it line the insides of his oesophagus as it slid down to his intestines. I gagged again, as did others.

Still with my eyes closed, I listened as Billy gagged violently before he threw the concoction back up, along with foul smelling stomach bile. I didn't dare open my eyes for fear of seeing the mixture lying centre stage of the putrid puke. Billy heaved again and there was another splash of sick splattering upon the tiled floor.

Someone else gagged and even I retched violently again, although I was able to keep down what was inside. So far at least.

'Easy money, huh?'

The man with the clipboard laughed.

'Not for you though.'

I kept my eyes closed but I knew he was talking to me. Heavy disdain in his voice.

'I told you, for everything you can't do for yourself, you lose ten thousand pounds. You're now down to just over sixty thousand and guess what… Whether you play the games by choice, you're still going to have to be a part of them.' He laughed. 'Come.'

Eyes still shut, I heard him start to walk away as the group continued gagging over what had been seen. I felt a vice-like grip grab my arm for a second time and I was dragged down the corridor towards wherever I was being led.

I just want this day to be over.

I hear a door open ahead of where I am being pulled but I still refuse to open my eyes. The smell of sick clings to me. I'm not sure if my eyes water because of that or because of genuine tears.

3.

'Open your eyes.'

I opened them in a hope that, in being compliant, they may be more lenient towards me. I was in a room of similar size to the last one. There is plastic sheeting on the floor around a table in the centre of the room. Beneath the sheeting, and underfoot now, the floors are white. The walls are covered in the same style sheeting laid upon the floor. I think the sight of it on the walls is worse. I can understand a mess on the floor, where they no doubt want me to do the tasks but on the walls a good few feet away? It hints towards splatter.

Tucked behind the table, there is a single chair. All around the table, standing tall on tripods, are a number of cameras pointing towards the chair. I'm not sure of the reason but my heart skips a beat when I see these. Most likely because it suggests I am to be filmed doing what is asked.

I looked at the man with the clipboard. I had a hope that my pathetic, worried look would be enough for him to feel some pity towards me. His blank expression suggests he feels none and, once again, I find myself yearning to be in the company of my bastard husband.

'Why are you doing this?' I asked him.

He didn't answer.

'Take a seat,' he said.

I momentarily find myself thinking about running once more but my feet are rooted to the spot. My legs still shake.

'Take a seat,' he said again. 'I won't be asking for a third time.'

I wonder what will happen if I refuse. I'm not refusing to do a task, just refusing to sit down. Could he dock more of the cash from what I am to potentially earn? It's not worth the risk. I've already lost ten thousand pounds for something which should have been the easiest, of all the things asked.

I walk to the table, pull the chair away from it and take a seat. I put my shaking hands on the cold metal table if only to stop them from shaking. Or rather to stop it being so obvious that they *are* shaking.

There's no harm in asking, 'Is there really nothing I can do to stop this?'

He shook his head. I expected nothing less. He doesn't say the words which are obvious: *I had every opportunity to leave.*

I asked, 'What are the cameras for?'

The second man stepped forward and pulled a laminated card from his pocket. He handed it to me and I scanned the words written upon it.

'What's this?'

'When the cameras record, you will read this out whilst looking straight down the lens of any of the cameras.'

I scanned the card again. I'm to give my name and tell the cameras, all that I do in the show is through my own choice. I have to say I that I wasn't forced to do any of it and was given plenty of chance to leave, should I have found any of the tasks to be too much.

I looked to the cameras again and, once more, asked, 'What is all of this for?'

'We are making a show. Have been for some time now. It's a Pay-Per-View show called *The Game*. We have been running it for a while now and our audience is growing somewhat.' He continued, 'We get people like you, Average Joes looking to make a quick bit of cash, and get them to take part in challenges whilst people at home watch. Not just that, they place bets online as to whether you're going to be able to do everything that is asked or whether someone will have to step in and do it for you.'

I looked from camera to camera and then back to the man with the clipboard who was still talking, not that I was really hearing his words at this point. My back was still sweating but now my armpits were tingling too as they also started to sweat.

'You're lucky,' he said. 'We're actually looking at changing the format over the coming months. At the moment we go out weekly but we're looking at staggering it a little further and having competitors going head to head, live for the paying public. Only one of them will win a prize that they'll love. The other gets nothing. This version of *The Game* is definitely easier for you to walk away with something if the rumours of the new version are even remotely close to being true.'

I don't feel lucky.

'You should breathe a sigh of relief. Like I said though, I've only heard rumours to the new format. My last day today so they're not telling me much although I'm kind of hoping for a Season Pass so I can still watch it, even if I'm not helping to organise it.' He turned to the man standing with him. 'Sure you'll sort that for me though, right?'

The other guy laughed even though I don't understand the joke.

'I'll see what I can do,' he told him.

I looked back to the cameras and found myself wondering how many people would actually want to watch something like this.

'People really watch it?'

'Are you kidding? If this was on Prime Time television, we would have the lion's share of the audience. You remember those old home-video shows where viewers submitted tapes of themselves doing dumb shit? They only stopped airing because there are only so many times we can watch someone fall over. *This* is what the audience wants though. They want to see people doing gross things for money. They want to see how far people will go... It's really all quite fascinating, seeing the figures people come up with to do this stuff. Like, did you know you were one of the cheapest people we've had? I can't remember the last time we had a contestant do this for under *£100,000.*'

There it was again; that feeling of sick trying to spew up from my stomach. I swallowed hard and tried to ignore both the feeling and the fact I had sold myself cheap.

All this just to escape a shitty marriage? I felt like a fool.

'Anyway you're probably keen to get this started. The sooner we begin, the sooner we finish and you get to go home a...' He cut his sentence short. 'I mean it's hard to call you a *rich* girl.' He shrugged. 'You get to go home better off than you were when you first came.'

I wiped a tear from my cheek as it snaked its way down from my eye. I didn't know what to say. I knew there was nothing that I *could* say. At least, nothing to stop this from happening. As he had made it clear several times, I had plenty of time to stop all of this. All I had to do was bow out when they kept asking. I chose to stay though. For why I have no idea. This was my choice and now I had to see it through.

'So this is how it is going to be. We will step out of the room. The cameras will start up. You will see red lights come on. That shows they're recording. Once you see that, you'll read the statement out loud and then set the card down. One of us will then bring in whatever is needed for the first task. Okay?'

It wasn't okay. None of this was okay. Still, I found myself nodding along like a compliant volunteer.

'Oh and because I'm feeling generous, I won't deduct the *£10,000* for failing to spit in that guy's face. Rest assured though, if you refuse to do anything else, I will take the money from you without hesitation. Normally I wouldn't even be this generous but, you know, it's my last day and I'm feeling kind.'

I feel like I should thank him but the words don't come out. How can I thank someone who is going to be making me do all these things? Yes I had the chance to leave but I've also begged to go home now too.

I give it one last ditch attempt to get out of this. 'There's nothing I can say to stop this from happening now, is there?'

He shook his head.

'Let the games commence,' he said.

4.

Having given my statement with a voice barely audible, I set the laminated card down on the metal table and pushed it to one side. I'm not sure if I read it out correctly, to the standards they wanted but the camera lights still show as recording so, I guess it was good enough. They're probably thankful I managed to get the words out in the first place, such was the squeakiness in my tone.

My heart was still racing. My back was drenched in sweat. My armpits felt wet. I was visibly shaking. My eyes were watery as hell and - from where I was trying not to cry - I occasionally felt my bottom lip quiver. In short: I was a wreck. The viewers, watching from wherever these sick fucks watched from, must have been able to tell that the statement in itself was forced, let alone what I was about to do. How could this show be allowed? How had it not been shut down and the people behind it prosecuted? None of it made sense to me.

I looked towards the door with, I'm sure, fear written all over my face as it opened and the quieter of the men came in with a jug of gravy in one hand and a pint glass in his second. Without a word, and staying out of the cameras' view, he set the items down on the table and made a retreat.

'What if I need to be sick?' I called out to him just before he left the room but he didn't wait to answer me. He disappeared, closing the door behind him.

The plastic sheeting surrounding me was the answer. If I needed to be sick, the plastic was there to protect the flooring.

I noticed they gave me nothing to cover my clothes though. They probably think I'll have enough money to go and buy myself something fresh to wear. I laughed to myself. All these internal thoughts pulling me away from the task at hand.

I looked at the gravy.

A brown concoction. It measured a pint exactly according to the measurements written upon the side of the jug. I picked it up and gave it a sniff. Beef gravy with no hidden surprises, from what I could tell. With a still shaking hand, I poured it into the pint glass. There was a small part of me which wondered what would happen if I accidentally got some on the floor. Would they let me get away with drinking what was left or would there be more waiting outside in case of such an accident? Knowing the money at stake and the willingness they seemed to have to want to take said cash away from me, I decided not to push my luck.

Once the jug was empty, I set it back down on the table and turned my attention to the glass.

As I poured the gravy out, I could see that it had gone lumpy over the time it had been left out. Worse, there was a skin formed on the top which had now disappeared to the bottom of the pint glass after transferring it. I knew that, once I started drinking, I'd have that "skin" to look forward to. My stomach twisted into yet another uncomfortable knot.

'Okay, it's just gravy.'

I picked the glass up and tilted the contents towards me. It was almost tar-like in its consistency. I closed my eyes. Immediately I was back at school where we had to clear our plates before we were allowed to leave the dining hall. An old trick came to mind whenever sprouts were dished up. You were supposed to hold your nose and close your eyes before you put them in your mouth. It was meant to stop you from being able to taste them although it never seemed to work for me. Even so, it never stopped me from trying this method when the time came to eat them.

With my spare hand, I gripped my nostrils shut. A slight hesitation and I started to tip the contents into my mouth. It didn't so much as pour into my mouth rather than land with a squelchy splatter. The weight pressed my tongue down a little and my mind instantly betrayed me as I found myself wondering as to whether the weight was the same as the thick phlegm spat onto Billy's tongue.

I gagged.

I tipped a little more in and then swallowed it as best as I could before it was too much to realistically get down without chucking it right back up again. At the back of my throat I felt the lumps push on through as they went on to slip down my gullet. All the time, I couldn't help but think about the phlegm in Billy's mouth.

I gagged again and, this time, retched too. I sat forward in my seat, worried that more was about to happen and that I was going to throw up.

Was that why Billy had been forced to take the spit in his mouth like that? Was it just a way of making my own brain play tricks on me? I tried to push it all from my mind. It's just gravy. Nothing more and nothing less.

Next mouthful.

I hesitated.

If anything this was worse despite knowing what to expect. I guess the first one wasn't quite as bad because I wasn't sure what it was going to actually be like. Once I knew how disgusting it was, it made it that little bit harder? Maybe?

I tipped the contents in and a second dollop landed heavy on my tongue. I tried to think of a food that I liked, which had the same feeling in the mouth, but nothing came to mind. Just thick-custard-like snot, curdled milk, grilled cheese rolled into a ball… I gagged and a little of the gravy spat out and hit my chin. Such was the thickness, it didn't trickle away. It stayed on the spot and proceeded to dry.

I swallowed hard and my throat made a *gulp* noise as the lumps pushed through once more. My stomach gurgled in protest as the first dollop landed within.

I don't dare open my eyes.

I don't dare see how much more I have to chug down.

I quicken my pace, desperate to get this over with.

Desperate to get this whole day over with.

As I tipped in the next mouthful, I kept thinking about the money and all that I could do with it. The thought was short-lived. Soon enough I was thinking about what I'd be doing next. A terrible thought which made the swallowing of the gravy even harder still.

I hope the viewers are enjoying this.

I hope they die.

5.

My top was cold. I'm sure it was probably a little see-through too. I had tried to get the vomit onto the plastic sheeting only but it had caught me by surprise. One minute I had a mouthful of gravy. The next I swallowed it and, immediately, the sick came up. It went down my top and a little into my lap. Not much hit the plastic sheeting ironically.

I must have looked pathetic. My eyes were streaming as I looked up to the man standing to the side of one of the cameras. Even he was looking a little sorry for me and yet he still held the spoon out for me to take from him.

I was reluctant but what were my choices? Do it and get it done so I can move on or have someone force-feed it to me and lose out on some of the money. Either option wasn't great but, if it was going in my mouth anyway, I'd sooner be paid for doing so.

I took the spoon from him and made the mistake of looking at what was smeared on it. A mass of yellowy-brown crap. It looks soft. I'm not sure if that is a blessing or a curse. A hair sticks out from it and I dread to think where it has come from. Was it pulled out from the backside as the crap pushed past? Was it there - a stray hair - from whomever had prepared my *treat*? I closed my eyes to it and tried to shut my mind down too. I didn't want to think about it, I said. Yet here I am.

'You have to eat it. Not just swallow it.'

I opened my eyes and looked at the man who had handed me the spoon. He was doing over the top chewing motions.

'They want to see you eat it. Really chew down on it.'

I looked back at the spoon. A shiver ran down my spine as I imagined doing exactly what he said. Never mind swallowing this, I wanted the ground to open up and swallow me. I can't remember who said it from the group but they raised a good point on how there were movies where people ate the end product of who they were with. Maybe it's just the thought of it which is disgusting? Maybe, in reality, it's not that bad?

Without further hesitation, I put the spoon in my mouth and scraped the product from it with my front teeth. It stuck to them and although my tongue hadn't touch upon it yet, I could tell that it *was* that bad. The people who ate it in the videos were either paid a lot, or freaks. I'm not sure which.

I set the now-clean spoon down on the table and licked the shit from my teeth. I gagged and promptly belched soon after that. It was so soft, I wasn't entirely sure how I was supposed to chew it. Not that I wanted to. For the sake of the cameras, I pretended to regardless even though it was still stuck to my tongue.

It's weird but the gravy, coupled with my imagination, was worse than this. Not that this is pleasant. I gagged again. I belched. My stomach ached. I knew this was going to need help getting down my throat though so I sucked some saliva into my mouth before I swirled it around. The taste suddenly became so much worse as the muck tainted my saliva.

My stomach knotted and I swallowed hard, desperate to get this over and done with and wishing for a breath-mint.

Once the mixture was gone, even though the taste lingered, I looked straight down the camera. I tried my hardest to look unfazed but knew I wasn't kidding anyone.

What are they doing? The people watching. What are they doing as they watch all of this? Are they laughing? Are they getting off on it? Are they not really paying attention and, in actual fact, I'm going through this for nothing?

My stomach cramped and I leaned over to the side. As I do, I bring up the rest of the gravy. A heavy mass of brown splatters the floor. It was just as lumpy coming out as it was, going in.

The residual taste in my mouth made me throw up again.

The door opened and the same asshole as before walked in. I wiped the dribble from my chin. My heart skipped a beat when I saw what was in his hand. He placed the handgun on the table before me.

'Safety is off,' he warned me.

The door opened for a second time. I leaned around the asshole to see what was happening. Silently, in single file, my fellow contestants walked back in. All of them looked concerned as they lined up against the wall.

'What's this?' I asked.

'Questions four and five.'

I looked at the gun. 'It's real?'

'What did you expect?'

'I don't know?'

'This is why we kept everyone back. Can't very well shoot them if we had let them go home.'

I noticed the cameras weren't recording anymore.

'You just need to choose someone out of the line-up and then they'll sit with you. When the cameras start back up you point the gun and pull the trigger. We don't mind which way round you do it. Take the bullet first, give the bullet first. So long as two bullets are fired and two people are shot, that's fine. Oh, and for the sake of argument, one of those people obviously needs to be you.'

I looked at the others. All of them looked ghostly pale.

'I can go to prison for this.'

'No. We have connections. That, and it will be made very clear to the viewers at home that everyone involved has been compensated heavily for this and is doing it by choice. You have nothing to worry about.'

'Apart from the pain of getting shot and knowing I'm shooting someone?'

The man shrugged.

'You can't be that worried about shooting someone,' he said. 'You put down that you'd do it for five pounds.'

I swallowed hard. A little acid burned the back of my throat as I thought back to filling in the form. I'd really put that little amount down? Maybe I had meant to add more zeros but got distracted?

I looked back to the others. Some of them looked shocked at the value I'd entered. Others didn't. I can only imagine what they put down but the guilt at my own figure ate away at me.

I don't know what I had been thinking. Even if Andrew and his tart had been standing before me, and I had a loaded gun, I wouldn't have pointed it at them, let alone pulled the trigger.

'So who is it going to be?'

'I can't kill anyone,' I said. My voice quaked as I fought back yet more tears.

'Is that what you think we're asking you to do?' He looked shocked. 'And you put £5.00 down? So less than an hour ago, you were happy to put a bullet into someone, killing them in the process, for just a fiver? Really? So - what changed between then and now?'

'I don't know what I was thinking.'

Maybe I put the money down low to make up for higher figures I had put earlier. I don't know! But I knew I couldn't shoot anyone! I wasn't even sure if I could shoot myself.

'If you can't do it, we can get it done for you but you do lose £20,000 of the money already coming to you. Those were the rules you agreed to.'

The panic must have been clear on my face for him to say that and he must have known I was struggling to get my head around this one.

'I don't know what I am doing anymore,' I said. I explained, 'I only came here because my husband is cheating on me. Some cheap bitch in his office. He doesn't think I know but I've known for a while.' I couldn't stop. 'I just want to get away from him. I want to start my life over but I work part-time. My own hours were cut and I've not found anything else yet… I got the invite to come here to win the money and I figured I had nothing to lose. I thought, if I can get enough, I'd be able to leave him. We've been married for a while now and I'd get what I am entitled to but a windfall of money… It would help me set myself up again as a single, independent woman. That's all I want. I want to be by myself. I want to start again. In time, maybe, find someone who loves me for me.' He was just staring at me with a blank expression. 'I didn't think this through properly and I'm sorry.'

There was a moment's silence. I swear I could hear my heart beating hard in my chest.

'So who are you going to shoot?'

I looked at the line-up. I looked at the gun. Even after all he had put me through and the betrayal I felt, I wished he was here now. I wished Andrew was here, not to shoot but to rescue me from this nightmare.

'Ready to make a decision? We need to keep this moving. We all want to get home today,' he pushed me.

Home? Did I want to get home? A cheating husband there, betraying me and yet still expecting me to wait on him like a *Stepford Wife* and what else was waiting for me? Not much. Friends who were too busy to see me unless they needed something. A bank balance which looked unhealthy, with regular calls from people I owed money to chasing me up. Did I want to go home?

'Hello?' He looked at me. No doubt he was wondering if I had heard him.

'I'm ready,' I said.

Steven Gibson's Last Shift

A Contingency

Steven sat at the table in the small office. In front of him were Jennifer's figures written out clearly, broken down by section and showing the full amount owed. He had already told her that he would let her off the spitting question and give her the ten grand back, which he was supposed to deduct according to the rules. A moment of being *generous* as it was his last shift and he'd felt sorry for her for agreeing to all of this for *such* a difference in costs between her and the next closest person.

Her current figure stood at £71,015 but it couldn't stay that way now. He grabbed his Mont Blanc from the side of the table, next to his keyboard, and put a line through the sum. Beneath it he then wrote £61,015. He'd been generous before but he wouldn't do it again. Not after she'd refused to shoot someone.

Laura screamed and put her hands in the air in defence as Steven raised the gun towards her. Before she had a

chance to beg him not to pull the trigger, he fired. She
slammed back against the wall and dropped to the floor
with her hands up to her throat where the bullet had
penetrated. The others panicked around her, trying to
help but it was no good. The bullet had passed straight
through and the blood was spraying out like a Las
Vegas Fountain. She had less than a minute left in which
to panic.

'I think she's still alive,' Nate said as he pressed his
fingers to Jennifer's neck, checking for a pulse. He was
crouched down next to her. Moments earlier she had
used the gun on herself, as per the task, but instead of
shooting herself in the foot, or somewhere equally
"harmless", she had set the barrel to her head. 'She's
still alive!'

Steven looked at the remaining tasks to be completed.
Jennifer needed to knock back a shot of blood. She also
needed to cut off a finger and eat it and then of course
there was the homeless man and the cum drinking. Five
tasks which she might not be able to do of her own

accord so a potential deduction of £50,000 which took her winnings down to £11,015.

'Not much there for the taking,' Steven muttered to himself as there was a knock at his office door. Louder, he said, 'Enter.'

The door opened and Nate walked in.

'What are you knocking for? Technically this is your office now,' Steven said cheerfully.

'Not yet. Not until you clock off.'

'Fair.'

Nate closed the door behind him and took a seat on the sofa which lined the far wall of the office. With the table, the sofa and Steven's own desk and chair, there wasn't much room for anything else in the room but, it was comfortable enough for the amount of time actually spent in there.

'We got a progress report?' Steven asked.

'Surgery was a success but they don't know the extent of the damage. Apparently the bullet went straight through the one side so, she was a lucky girl indeed.'

'I wonder if she will think so.' Steven paused a moment. 'I wonder if she will be able to think.'

Nate shrugged. He wasn't a doctor so couldn't answer the question. To him, a bullet to the head was instantly fatal going by the many films he'd seen over the years. This was the first time he had heard of someone surviving such a shot but apparently it wasn't rare. It all depended on whether the bullet passed right through or whether it bounced around the skull causing more damage. Then of course there was a question of which *part* of the brain it hit. As the doctors said to Nate when he checked on her progress, she was a lucky girl indeed.

'As per your request, the cameras have been set up in her room but the doctors did advise to give her a little time to get over the trauma.' He added, 'She needs to rest and recover and...'

Steven turned in his chair to look at Nate. With a smile on his face he said, 'She doesn't need to recover. She just needs to get through to the end of the game and I've just been doing the maths now. Because she won't be in a state to do anything for herself, she will lose fifty grand. I've already been on the phone to the person who won the last contestant.'

'You have? Why?'

'You didn't know him but he was a crazy son of a bitch. Although not so crazy he walked away with less money than this woman but… He just didn't give a shit. The tasks asked of him? We were in that room less than two hours. He just rushed straight through them and asked if that was all there was once he was done.' Steven added, 'I called him up and asked how much it would cost us to get him to help us out a little.'

'And?'

'His rates were more than reasonable and it's still going to be one of the cheapest episodes we've ever aired. He's on his way now.'

'And he knows all he has to do?'

'Said it was easier than what we had made him go through and laughed down the phone. Told me to have the cash waiting for him. So, we'll give him what *she* loses plus a little extra and the audience gets a full show still.'

Nate was impressed. He wouldn't have thought to do any of that but that was where Steven's experience kicked in. Now he'd seen the way this had been handled though, Nate knew he could cope with such a problem if it were to arise again in the future.

'The bosses won't mind that you got someone else in?'

'Another lesson for you: They don't care so long as the show airs and doesn't cost more than the money earned from the viewing memberships.'

Steven reached for a file in the top drawer of his desk. He tossed it over to Nate who caught it, despite not expecting having anything thrown at him.

'What's this?'

'Viewing figures and membership details. All the financials for the last couple of months. You can see what comes in, you can see what goes out. As long as the income is more than the outgoings, the bosses will leave you be but we can go through all of that later.'

Nate was flicking through the pages within the file. It all seemed straight forward enough but he'd never turn down the chance to talk about it in more detail. He didn't just want to take over from Steven. There was an arrogant part of him which wanted to *better* what Steven had accomplished here. He wanted bigger bonuses for himself. He wanted more eyes on him. Employee of the fucking month. He wanted to be the best.

A telephone rang on Steven's desk. Steven turned back to his desk as Nate continued going through the figures. He lifted the phone from the receiver.

'Hello?'

Nate looked up from the paperwork. He wondered whether it was the doctors calling up about Jennifer.

'Okay. We're on our way.'

Steven hung the phone up and swivelled in his chair.

'It's showtime,' he said.

Stale Urine

Both Nate and Steven gagged as they walked into the room with the homeless man in it. He was sitting, waiting for the two men, as instructed by the woman on the reception desk. When he saw the two suited and booted men standing in the doorway, he couldn't help but show his confusion as to why he had been summoned.

Steven turned to Nate and said, 'He'll do. Make it happen.' With that, he left the room leaving Nate to talk to the homeless man. Out in the corridor, Steven could be heard retching.

The homeless man was in his fifties but looked older. Years on the street had been cruel. What few teeth he had were broken and stained yellow. His fingernails were so long they'd started to twist. Despite the length, they were cracked from years of scrambling through trash on the hunt for food or anything that could be used for his own survival.

And his scent?

He stunk of stale urine. One could only hazard a guess as to how many times he'd got so blind drunk that he'd pissed his pants whilst unconscious and, Nate couldn't help but recognise another smell, not just wet himself either. Fresh shit was also there, in the mix.

'How would you like to earn one thousand pounds?' Nate looked him up and down. He knew a grand to the old man was a lot of money and would be hard to refuse. But then, he could have probably got him to do the task for free. Looking at the state of him he'd probably not had sex for so long that his virginity would have grown back. Jesus. Could he even remember how to fuck?

The homeless man eyed him up suspiciously. He had been down on his luck for as long as he could remember now and when people did come along with promises of help, it was usually a cruel trick. Why would this time be any different? Something about city folk. They like to kick a person when they're already at their lowest. Some kind of sick game to them.

'What I got to do?'

'Fuck a woman.'

The homeless man couldn't help but look shocked. Of all the things this guy could have said, this was *not* what he had been expecting to come from his mouth.

'I'm confused.'

'No need to be. Would you fuck a woman for one thousand pounds, in cash? Come into the room where she is, climb on top, pound her hard, ejaculate, pull your pants up, take the cash and leave. That's it.'

'Does she know about this?'

Nate laughed. 'Does it matter?'

The homeless man fell silent for a minute.

'Can I have a shower or something?'

'It's not necessary,' Nate lied. 'She won't give a shit either way and we're running late. So. What do you say? Want to earn a grand?'

'Chuck in a sandwich and you have a deal.'

Nate laughed.

'Fuck her first and then we'll get you a sandwich on the way out.'

The homeless man shrugged.

'If you'd like to follow me.'

Nate turned from the homeless man and back towards the door. He stepped into the corridor half-expecting to find Steven standing there but he'd long gone. Perks of it being his last shift; he didn't have to deal with the stinking hobo. He'd had his fill of them throughout the years of working there and had decided to leave it all up to Nate. Nate knew what to do.

True enough, Nate led the way down the corridor towards the stairs. Jennifer's room was two floors up but there was no way he was going to get into the elevator with the stench following him. At least taking the stairs would allow more clean air and distance between them. And, as an added bonus, he'd get his step count up too. His *Apple Watch* would be proud.

Nate pulled one of the fire exit doors open and stepped from the corridor to the stairwell. He paused a moment to hold the door open for the man following and, then, led the way up the stairs.

'Can I ask why you chose me?'

'Does it matter?'

'Not really. Just curious.'

Nate decided to bend the truth. 'Why shouldn't people be given a treat occasionally, just because they're down on their luck? You were seen out there… It's been shitty weather recently… My colleague probably thought you deserved a break.'

'Not quite the break I need but I'm not complaining,' the man said. He laughed. His laugh was more of a cackle and reminded Nate of *The Cryptkeeper* from the old television show *Tales From The Crypt*. 'Is she pretty?'

Nate laughed and answered again, 'Does it matter?'

'Long as she has a pulse, I guess not.'

'She's got a pulse.'

'I'm good then.'

Nate didn't let on that the pulse was *barely* there. The old man would see for himself soon enough. He was kind of curious as to whether he'd go through with what was being asked though. Had the shoe been on the other foot, Nate wasn't sure he could. It would be different if the woman was conscious and consenting but in her state, Nate knew she would be neither. This wasn't sexual intercourse, it was rape. What kind of man was this walking up the stairs behind him? A kind man down on his luck or a monster lurking in the underbelly of society?

Two floors up and Nate opened the fire escape door. He stepped through to the next corridor with the man following closely behind.

'Almost there,' he said as he continued walking down the corridor towards the room Jennifer was being monitored in.

'I'm nervous,' the old man said with a laugh.

'No need to be.'

'It's been a while.'

'She won't care.'

'What if she doesn't like me?'

'She won't care.'

'What if I don't like her?'

'You don't have to marry her. The question should be, how much do you want to walk out of here with a thousand pounds?'

'And a sandwich.'

'And a sandwich,' Nate confirmed. Part of him wondered whether he could have bought the man for a few nights in a cheap hotel and a tray of sandwiches. Would have been cheaper. Still, he knew for next time. Start lower and if the offer is refused, let them haggle a little.

He stopped at the door to Jennifer's room.

'This is it.'

The old man joked, 'How do I look?'

Nate smiled, unsure what to say. He opened the door to reveal Jennifer lying in a bed, tubes poking out of her and various machines hooked up to her, sounding off with a series of beeps.

'What is this?' The homeless man looked from Jennifer to Nate, genuine concern on his face.

'This is Jennifer and,' he lied, 'you're her dying wish.'

'She's unconscious.'

'Now. When she asked for you, she was very much awake.'

They stepped into the room. The old man looked at her with sorrow in his eyes.

'What happened?'

'We're on a bit of a time limit. Does her life story really matter?'

'You want me to fuck a dying woman…'

'For a big chunk of cash.' He added, 'If it helps we can get in some Viagra.'

'What if I hurt her.'

'I don't think she will care either way at this particular moment in time.'

The man finally noticed the cameras around the room.

'What is this?'

'Her family are paying and want to know you did what you said you would do. They figured it would be off putting if they were here watching so they asked for us to film it.'

'And put the footage up on a porn site?'

'Sir, does it look like we're into making porn films with dying women?'

The hobo looked at Jennifer and around the room again.

'And if it does,' Nate added, 'does it really matter?'

Nate glanced at the mirror on the far wall. He knew Steven was in the next room, on the opposite side of the mirror watching. He could picture him laughing his arse off at the exchange between him and the homeless man and it took everything in him to stop from smiling himself.

'This is fucking crazy.'

'And worth a thousand pounds.'

'And a sandwich.'

'And a sandwich.' Nate asked, 'When was the last time you fucked someone?'

The old man didn't answer. He couldn't remember the exact date.

'Anyone going to be on the cameras?'

'They're controlled remotely.'

'Not sure I can perform with an audience.'

'No one else will be in the room.'

The guy didn't have the internet. There was no need to tell him about the number of viewers who'd be watching him complete one of Jennifer's tasks for her. And, with this task done, Louis Du Toit was already on the way to help with the others.

The hobo looked around the room, searching for something.

'Any rubbers?'

Nate laughed. 'Don't need them. She's clean.'

The old man laughed. 'Am I though?'

Nate winked. 'She doesn't care.' He waited a moment on the off-chance the old man was going to say something. No words came out. Instead, he simply licked his lips. Nate smiled. 'I'll leave you two to get better acquainted.' He added, 'I'll come by in about twenty minutes, see how you're getting on.'

Nate left the room before the hobo could waste any more time. He figured twenty minutes was plenty long enough for the old man to get it up, stick it to her and finish up. If it really had been that long since he'd fucked someone, he'd probably not even need half of that time. Still, what he didn't know was that both Nate and Steven would be watching from the other room.

The moment the door closed, the cameras lights lit up. *And action.*

A Heavy Load

Steven was standing at the glass, watching through to the homeless man fucking Jennifer. This brown, shit-stained arse bouncing up and down as the dirty fucker gave it his all.

'Even with the wall between us,' Steven said, 'I'm sure I can smell him still. That was fucking disgusting.'

He'd seen this enough times to have become a little desensitised to it now, unlike Nate who was standing in the corner of the room and refusing to watch. Steven couldn't take his eyes from the guy's arse. Even from this distance, he could see the hairs on it, all matted up and caked in crap. He didn't understand it. He knew life on the streets was tough but there were public toilets and even if you couldn't find one that was open, or that didn't charge - surely you'd just head down an alleyway and drop your cacks? You wouldn't just shit your pants, surely? He could only imagine how uncomfortable it was but that wasn't his only thought.

'She should probably be grateful that she's unconscious,' Steven continued. 'I saw the guy wasn't circumcised. Can you imagine the build up of smegma under that foreskin? I mean the guy reeks. Absolutely reeks. If he doesn't care about piss and shit, he probably doesn't care about cock-cheese.' He paused a moment before he turned to Nate. 'When he is done, might be worth asking him if we can get a sample of that by the way.'

'What?'

'A potential new question: How much to chew down on a tramp's built-up smegma?' He laughed. 'Make them put it in their mouth and suck it through their teeth. That kind of thing.' He added, 'It's a pity she isn't awake for this as we could have done it as a bonus. Peel back his foreskin and clean away the crusty cheese with your teeth. Scrape that shit away, roll it around in your mouth and swallow the tiny flakes down.'

'Is he done yet?'

Steven turned back to the glass partition. The old man was lying motionless on top of Jennifer who, obviously, hadn't moved.

'Or he is dead,' Steven said casually.

Nate walked from the corner and looked through the mirror.

'What's he doing?'

Trapped (bonus chapter)

Moments Earlier:

I wanted to scream when he walked into the room. I couldn't see him, but I could smell him. I wanted to beg them not to do this. I wanted to say that I had surely paid the ultimate price but - no words would come out and no notice would be given to me. To them, I am unconscious. I'm not though. I just look as though I am. Everything about me, mentally, is still - somehow - still firing on all cylinders despite my own wish that it wasn't.

An unknown man leaned down to me and sneered. The smell was truly hideous yet I could not even gag. I just had to lie there and breathe it in. Fish. Cheese. Vinegar. Chicken gone off. A combination of smells all laced heavily with piss and shit, mixed with the smell of wet clothes that had taken too long to dry.

'How long do I have?'

His breath was rancid too. Furry teeth and food debris squashed between his yellow-stained teeth. What teeth remained anyway. More gums than anything else.

'However long you need. We will leave you to it.'

'And I can do anything?'

'As long as you are fucking her like she wanted.'

He smiled. I wanted to gag. I couldn't.

I heard the door open and close again. We were alone. This man and I.

Now:

He grunts as he fucks me. The only saving grace to all of this is that I cannot feel what he is doing to my pussy. I cannot feel his dick inside of me. I just know it is and even that is bad enough as my imagination paints in the pictures and feelings and what it could be looking like and what it could be feeling.

I imagined his cock all brown and crusted in filth now looking clean and spotless thanks to scraping itself free of debris inside of me. All that filth that was once encrusted to him, now deep in me where it will continue to fester and putrefy until I have an infection. His finger nails are probably spotless now too… He'd held his fingers up to show me them earlier and beneath the nails was packed with black mud. Again, had I been able to gag I would have done so when he licked those fingers clean and put them between my legs. A small mercy that I couldn't feel them inside of me. His jagged nails cutting inside.

His grunts are getting louder now. His face directly in mine as he continues to breath yesterday's scrounged food directly into my face as he pumps his putrid cock in and out of me. I wish I could scream out. I wish I could call for help or demand he get off me.

I wish the bullet had killed me.

A Heavy Load (Part 2)

The homeless man had shot his load. A heavy shot of stinking cum straight up into the unconscious woman's snatch. He was just lying there with his cock still inside her. He was breathless but with a wide smile on his face. An early Christmas Day for him; one thousand pounds in the back pocket and a fuck. He laughed when he remembered the promise of the sandwich too.

He pulled his hips back slightly and let his softening cock slip out of her stretched cunt. A dollop of ejaculate slipped out with his dick and trickled down onto the mattress between her legs.

The door opened behind him suddenly as both Steve and Nate walked in. Despite leaving Nate to sort the man earlier, Steven took the lead this time.

'Yep. Okay. Thanks then. Pants up, collect your money and leave. Good job, my friend. Good friend. Oh, one thing… We would appreciate this staying between us. You know, don't go running off telling your homeless buddies down by the local trash cans. Who knows, if you keep it our little secret, maybe we'll use you again…'

The while he was talking, the old man climbed off the still body of Jennifer and was busy tucking himself back into his pants. He didn't bother wiping his cock clean beforehand, even though there was a little blood on it thanks to pushing into Jennifer dry and causing some internal ripping. But why would he worry about that when he was already caked in just about every other bodily juice you could imagine?

'And your mate said about a sandwich,' the man said.

Steven looked at Nate.

'I'll get your sandwich,' Nate said.

'And, you know, if you need any other near dead girls fucked - I'm your man.' He cackled again and, again, Nate was reminded of *The Cryptkeeper*.

'Sure,' Steven said.

Nate led the man towards the exit as Steven approached Jennifer. When it was just the two of them in there, he leaned towards her bandaged face and whispered to her, 'Technically you didn't *let* him fuck you so it doesn't count that he did. We'll be taking the money from you and we'll also be taking the money for the last few tasks too seeing as it's no good for the viewers if they're not getting a reaction. See, they're paying for the reaction. Watching some unconscious person having shit done to them? It's not fun. There's no sense of disgust or satisfaction in seeing them getting grossed out or whatever. So, you'll be pleased to hear - if indeed you can even hear… You're almost done and, if you wake up, you will be awarded the money you are owed. Unless of course you can't remember anything about this in which case I'll probably advise my colleague to just say you were mugged or something. Every penny saved, and all that. More money for the Christmas party.'

He stood up straight and couldn't help but notice the semen trickling from her ruined cunt. His expression turned to one of disgust; even the homeless man's spunk looked tainted a browny-yellow colour. He almost felt a little sorry for Louis. It was him who was going to have to deal with this, after all. But then, after what he did, it would probably be a breeze in the park.

As the memory raced back through Steven's mind, he shuddered. He had seen a lot in his time with the company and most of what he had seen had been his fault. It was, after all, his suggestions as to what was turned into the *How Much To* questions. The only time he'd really felt sick though, like properly *sick,* was when he had watched Louis Du Toit.

My Name Is Louis Du Toit

1.

I closed my eyes because, quite frankly, I didn't need a close-up inspection of the bastard's winking asshole. I set my mouth against the dirty, stretched ring like I was playing a fucked-up musical instrument and, as instructed, I sucked as hard as I could. The whole time I did so, I imagined I was sucking on a supermodel's pussy. At least I tried. The taste of the initial sweat wasn't doing much to help my imagination. Unless of course said supermodel had just got off a busy shift on the catwalk?

At first, other than the taste of sweat, which was mostly made up of salt, there was nothing of note to really taste. I sucked harder but, still, there was nothing.

I pulled away and opened my eyes, looking at the chocolate starfish. My first mistake of the day. A little trickle of jizz and liquified shit had made its first appearance. Had I just sucked once more, instead of pulling away to look, the image would never have entered my mind and, instead, I would just be tasting it now. I just hope that the strawberry lube I used to penetrate him makes up the majority of what I am to taste but, given how the salty sweat was so evident, I doubt I'll be so lucky.

I looked towards the camera recording me and winked.

'In for a penny, in for a pound.'

Or, in my case, a couple of hundred thousand pounds.

I set my mouth back against his hole and sucked hard again. As I did so, he seemed to push back against my face so that my nose disappeared up his crack. Not the best place to be but, I sucked harder, hopefully I won't be here long.

The taste hit home and it took my all not to pull away and throw it up. A little of our mixed concoction had touched the taste buds of my tongue. It tasted of iron, cabbage, salt. The texture was similar to a lumpy yoghurt. I don't want to know what the lumps are given how hard I've sucked direct from his colon and I refuse to stop to take another look.

A couple more hard sucks and my mouth felt full of "gravy". I turned to the camera, breathing hard through my nose, and opened my mouth for the viewers to see. I stuck my tongue out for them. It felt coated as though I'd given it a paint job. No longer pink, I bet it's now brown and rancid looking. A few seconds later and I pulled my tongue back into my mouth, tilted my head back and swallowed. I shuddered as my mouth emptied and gullet filled.

'We done?'

I looked at the homeless man. He was still on all fours. He was looking back at me whilst stroking his cock.

I smiled. Teeth, brown.

'We are done,' I said.

Time to get paid.

*

Eating the cummy pussy was easier than sucking my own load out of another guy's arsehole. While I couldn't say I enjoyed the taste of his mixture, at least I was able to push my tongue deeper into her to get a taste of her too and that was what I was concentrating on. The taste of her sweet pussy.

I had licked her so long now that she was all I could taste. The man-juice had already been licked up and devoured but I didn't want *them* to know this so occasionally I pretended as though I were struggling. In truth, I was just getting off on this now and I wished they had called me sooner so that I could have been the one to fuck her. I wonder, would they let me have a go on her too if I suck out my own cum as well? Same rules as before? Looking at her, I'm not sure whether they can put her on her front - what with all the tubes poking from her. But if they could, I'd happily eat her colon out for free.

After a few more laps of her labia, I pulled away and smiled to the camera.

'Yummy.'

I got up from between her legs and positioned myself on the edge of her bed for what would come next. One task down and three more to go.

'Let's do this,' I said, keen to both get it over and receive the handsome payday I was promised. The camera's red light stopped recording.

The door opened and Steven stepped into the room. He was smiling from ear to ear.

'Really giving them a show,' he said.

I smiled at him. 'You know me.' With that, I waved my arm stump at him. A million pounds to wave my arm into a spinning circular saw. I might have passed out the moment the blade sliced through flesh, tissue, muscle and bone but - when I'd woken up - I didn't bitch about it. Through the drugs they'd given me for the pain, I just asked what was next.

'And this is why I called you,' he said to me.

'What's next then?'

'We're going to move you into the room originally set up for Jennifer. It's all good to go with everything you need on the table so, you can go as quickly as you want through the tasks. Then, at the end, we'll have your money waiting for you.' He added, 'Follow me.'

Steven left the room and I followed as instructed. It was weird seeing him again. I thought, after the last time, I would never see him again. In truth, I'm not sure how I feel *about* seeing him. I lost a lot, the day we met. But on the flip-side, I also earned a lot so I couldn't really complain.

As he led the way, I made small chat.

'So how have you been?'

'Well, thank you.'

'That's good then. And clearly things are going well with you here,' I said.

'Last day today.'

'You're shitting me?'

'No. Moving on.'

'Can't believe it.'

'Believe it. The other guy who came to meet you with me; that's my replacement. Nice enough guy but maybe too nice for the job? Who knows. Time will tell.'

'What's next? Mass executions?'

Seriously - where do you go after a job like this?

He laughed at my suggestion.

'No. I'm moving to the music industry.'

'What?'

I heard what he said, and he knew I had so he didn't bother repeating himself. It was more of a *what* like, how in the fuck can you go from this to working in the music industry.

'If you honestly believe the music industry isn't as sadistic as this one, you're sadly mistaken,' he said. 'I have some great ideas on how to move forward there too,' he said.

'Really? Like what?'

He looked at me - still walking forward - and smiled.

'I could tell you,' he said, 'but then I would have to kill you.'

'Guess I'll have to wait and see,' I said. 'Maybe you'll let loose with some of your secrets when you're interviewed by *N.M.E.*'

He laughed again. 'Maybe.'

We walked in silence for a moment.

'What about you?'

I asked, 'What about me?'

'Have you spent the money yet?'

'Not yet but I could do with a top up.'

'Hence you're here again.'

'Well when you said what needed to be done… I'm sorry but these questions seemed easier than what I had to go through.'

'They're harder in a different way. All depends on what you can stomach. I'd rather cut something off than do all the eating shit.'

I shrugged. I'd do anything so long as the price was right.

He stopped by a door and pulled it open.

'After you.'

I walked into the room. It was similar to one he'd made me use before. Fairly small. A table in the centre with plastic sheeting on the floor. Cameras set up all pointed to a chair that was next to the table.

'That's new,' I said.

I pointed towards the puddle of sick on the floor and to the splattering of blood towards the back wall.

'No sense cleaning things up when we'll only be back here cleaning up again later, right?'

I shrugged. I mean, it would have been nice to have a clean room but, there you go.

The door opened behind us and the same guy I'd been introduced to earlier came in with a covered tray. He took the tray over to the table and set it down.

'Everything there?' Steven asked.

The other guy, I forget his name, nodded.

'And the other contestants?'

'Signed the paperwork, took some compensation and left.'

'The *other* girl.'

'Back of a van ready to be dropped off.'

I guess they'd already killed someone. I'm not surprised. A couple of people died by my hands - well, when I had *hands* - when I was doing the game.

The guy continued, 'The hardest thing was finding the homeless guy a fucking sandwich.'

Steven laughed. I had no idea why but I laughed along with them.

'You've already been here longer than you should have been because of her operation,' the guy said. 'Did you want to get out of here? I can finish up.'

'It's fine. Anyway, I want to see how my friend Louis does,' Steven said as he looked at me with a smile.

'Are we friends?' I asked him.

He patted me on the back and said, 'You did what was asked of you, you didn't hang about in getting it done and you are back to help us out of a tricky situation now.' He added, 'We're friends.'

I looked at my arm stump. I'd hate to see what he did to people he didn't class as being a friend.

'So,' he said, 'you know what needs to be done?'

I nodded.

'The shot, the finger, the finger food,' he said.

'I know.'

I walked over to the table and took a seat, careful not to put my foot in the sick.

'Jesus,' I said, 'what the fuck did she eat? This shit is rife.'

I couldn't help but to glance down at the mess. There were small lumps of carrot, clumps of some kind of mixture and fuck knows what else puddled there. I closed my eyes to it and turn away. When I opened my eyes again I tried to focus on something else and forget what they'd made me do before.

*

I put my fingers down my throat and rimmed around the throat-hole, whatever the fuck the proper term for that is. Immediately I retched. I pressed against my tonsils again and, again, I retched. This time though the retching led onto more violent gagging and I felt my stomach clench and then convulse. A moment later and I sprayed a reeking fountain of brown stomach bile over my hand and clothes. Not good. I had completely missed the glass I was aiming for. I repeated the process; poking the back of my throat with my fingers. More sick. This time I had more success in getting it into the glass. It didn't fill it up but there was more than enough for the necessary requirements.

I paused a moment to catch my breath. Throwing up, even through choice - not that it's a choice I tend to make often, really takes it out of me. I sat there a moment, kind of dazed. My eyes were transfixed on the little red light on the front of the camera. Rather look there than the glass of sick I was about to drink back. All these people watching me. I wonder if they're enjoying the show? I hope so. I'm going to enjoy spending the money.

I swallowed hard.

There was a strong acidic taste. I try and push it from my mind because, fair to say, it's about to get a hell of a lot worse.

'Here we go,' I said.

Eyes fixed on the camera, I tipped the glass of vomit back into my mouth. The gag reflex kicked in immediately and it took everything I had not to spray the shit back out and bring up even more in the process. Quickly I swallowed. It wasn't just smooth liquid that went down. There were stringy bits too.

I vomited it right back out again, straight down my front. I gasped for a breath and then, I sicked up again. It didn't matter how much came out though. I gasped for air again and threw up for a third time. I had done what was asked. I had swallowed it. All of it. The stringy bits of whatever the fuck that was; some of which was now stuck between my teeth. The lumps of carrot, even though I'd not eaten any… I threw up again.

Stop fucking thinking about it.

*

'Okay you know what happens. We will leave the room. The camera lights will start flashing so you know you're being recorded. From there, you can go at your own pace. If you pass out, the recordings will stop. We will bring you back around and - from there - you can go again.'

'I know the rules.'

'Well then, we will leave you to it.'

Steven walked to the door with his colleague. I watched as they both left. I turned to the mirror behind me. Any minute now and they'd be standing there, watching my progress. I never did understand why they didn't set the room up so they could watch a person head on but, each to their own.

From over my shoulder, I heard the cameras start to whirl. I turned back, facing forward. The cameras were flashing red.

Here we go again.

3.

I removed the cover from the tray. Nothing on it was a surprise. There was a small guillotine-type tool so that I could remove a finger; a fair compromise to take the digit off given the fact I only have one arm since the last time I was here. Can't exactly use a cleaver to cut a finger off my other hand, given how I have no idea where that hand is anymore.

Next to the finger-cutting device, there's a shot glass filled with blood. At least that was what they said it was. It doesn't look like blood. At least, not fresh blood. I'm unsure whether it is human claret or from an animal. I'm guessing it doesn't really matter though, right? Blood is blood.

The blood is dark red and looks clotted, like a blackcurrant jelly. Other than that, the tray is empty. Really it doesn't look like much. I sit back there a moment and mentally try to work out in which way to do this.

So I have to lose a finger. I have to drink the blood. I have to eat the finger I choose to remove. Logic would say that I should remove the finger and then eat it. The blood I can do at the same time. Something wet to wash the finger down with.

Okay.

Here we go, said the ear-wig.

I put my finger through the small hole of the guillotine-type machine. Next, I rested my chin against the handle of the blade. I took a couple of deep breaths and…

I rammed downwards. The blade sliced through the finger with ease. The pain was instant and I screamed as my finger plopped off into a small bucket in front of the device. I stopped screaming and sucked in some air through my teeth. Slowly, trying to compose myself, I let it out before taking a look at the damage done by the blade. My little finger was cut clean off. Looking down into the wound, I could see the bone. Given all I'd done to myself before, I was surprised to see little spots appear in my vision. I blinked my eyes a few times until the spots disappeared. A few more deep breaths.

I picked the finger up. Now I wouldn't normally use my pinky to pick something small up and obviously I didn't now, what with it not being attached to my hand. But it feels alien, using my hand and picking something up now that I'm missing a digit.

The finger is only small but not so small that I think I'd be able to swallow it in one, which is unfortunate. I hold it between my thumb and index finger like it's a small chicken wing.

That's all it is.

It's just a chicken wing.

I just need to eat the skin and flesh away of the wing. No problem. I do it every time I order a pizza: One large pizza and a side of wings. And I strip those fuckers of meat within seconds so, this is just the same as that but, I expect, a little tougher.

I put the finger to my lips. It was still warm. I parted my lips and clenched my teeth against the flesh. All I need to do is break the skin and pull the meat away. I can do this... Just eat enough of the flesh to get the whole thing a little smaller and then - swallow what remains. Wash it down with the shot of blood.

I bit down. My teeth pierced the skin easier than I had expected. I pulled back with my head and ripped the finger away with my hand; tearing the skin off in the process. Much easier than I imagined although, with the flesh in my mouth, I realised how tough it actually was as I started to chew down on it.

Usually I'm fairly polite when it comes to eating. I cannot stand people who eat with their mouths open, showing anyone and everyone what they're eating and forcing them to watch it go round and around in their mouths. All the foods mushed up, squelching around… Little bits of spittle flying out and landing here and there. Not today though. Today I was one of the people I despise as I chewed with my mouth open, hoping to let some of the taste escape before my senses kicked in.

I swallowed with a strain. I hadn't chewed enough but, I *had* chewed more than I wanted to. I brought the finger back up to my mouth and repeated the process. Knowing how tough it was, once in the mouth, I bit off a little less this time which, in itself, was easier.

Chew.

Chew.

Chew.

Swallow.

Bite.

Chew.

Chew.

Chew.

Gag.

Swallow.

Bite.

Chew.

Chew.

Chew.

Chew.

Swallow.

I looked at what remained of my finger. It was small enough so, without stopping to overthink anything, I place it in my mouth and grabbed the shot of blood. I closed my eyes, tipped my head back and poured the shot in, alongside the finger. It's just jam and ham. That's it. An odd combination but nothing strange or disgusting about that.

I sat up straight and swallowed hard. The lumps in the blood were nothing but clumps of squashed fruits. That's all. The bone of the finger, and hanging pieces of flesh... Just a cocktail sausage half-masticated and full of gristle. It caught as it disappeared down my throat and I couldn't help but to cough. Thankfully it was just a cough though and I didn't spit any of it back out. As soon as my mouth was empty, I opened it for the sake of the camera and viewers at home. *All empty now.*

I sat back in the chair. My hand was throbbing. My mouth tasted disgusting. But I had done it. For the second time I had played their games and I had done what was required. I don't know why - maybe nervous energy? - but I started to laugh.

The red lights on the camera switched off.

Feeling lightheaded, I turned in my chair and looked towards the mirror. I raised my hand and, with a cocky smile, gave the people behind it a confident thumbs up.

'What we doing next time then?'

And That's A Wrap

Steven was laughing as he watched Louis through the mirror. Nate wasn't laughing but couldn't take his eyes from him.

'The guy is insane,' Nate said.

Steven nodded.

'And that would be why I called him,' he said.

'Can I take his number from you in case I need him again?'

'All in the files.' Steven turned away from the mirror. 'I'm sorry today didn't go exactly as planned but it's probably for the best as you got to see it play out as a worst case scenario. The important thing to take away from the day is; whatever happens, footage is filmed and available to upload to the subscribers. No footage and you may as well film yourself doing whatever it is lined up because, trust me, that is what will happen.'

'No shit.'

'Any questions so far?'

Nate shrugged. It had been more than a long day. With waiting for Jennifer to come out of the operating theatre, it was knocking closer to three days. He was tired. He was hungry and his head felt as though it were going to explode with all that he'd seen and been through.

'Honestly I have no idea,' he said. 'I'm sorry your last shift wasn't as easy as it should have been.'

'You kidding? I had a blast. I'm almost going miss this place.'

'Can stay on and give me some more guidance? Use some of the money saved from the first woman to pay yourself an extra couple of days' wages?'

Steven laughed.

'Thanks but no thanks. Anyway, there'll be giving you more training. You were never going to be able to take everything in on the first day.'

'Yeah. I see that now.'

Nate looked back through the mirror. Louis was standing up, stretching his back and trying to shake the pain away from his hand.

'So what happens now?'

Steven stood next to Nate by the window.

'Well,' he said, 'now I am going to go home. You're going to pay the man. You're going to clean the mess up and then tomorrow you're going to come back at a sensible hour and write in all the figures and file a report on what happened. Once that's done, you're going to upload the footage and start to plan the next show. Rinse, repeat, rinse, repeat…' He added, 'And if that bitch survives the bullet through the brain, you're going to pay her too.' He paused a moment and then laughed. 'Just don't forget to deduct the medical costs.'

Nate realised the full weight of the role he had taken on in that instance.

'You sure you don't have room for me in your new music job?'

'Afraid not.' Steven laughed. 'Tell you what though, when I create my first artist for the mainstream… To show I'm thinking of you and our time together here - I'll name him after you, Nate.'

Nate looked at him, unsure if he was taking the piss.

'That's kind of you.'

Steven laughed and patted him on the shoulder.

'You did good today.'

With that, he walked from the room leaving Nate to his own thoughts. His eyes scanned the mess in the next room; vomit on the floor, blood and sick on the table, blood on the walls…

Did he really have to clean this shit up? An operation that big and they didn't have cleaners to come by and help with all of this?

He sighed.

It had been a long first shift and, looking at the mess next door, it was going to be an even longer night.

The Contestants

Michelle Ehrhardt, Trudy Russell, Simone Moriarty, Audra Walgenbach, Steven Edwards, Dean Watts, Svenja Böttle and Billy Smith

With the paperwork signed, stating they wouldn't discuss the events of the day with anyone, the contestants went about their lives with a little extra money in their back pockets. Whilst it wasn't the amounts they had hoped to win, it was still enough to ensure their silence was bought and that they would be able to enjoy themselves a little or, at the very least, pay for therapy after the day's events.

Whilst most moved on and went about their lives as quietly as they could, wary of accepting further invitations posted out to them, a couple had a more tragic ending.

Billy Smith ended up leaving the biker's club, unable to ride after his accident. Soon after the club was raided by the authorities with most higher up members charged with various felonies. Despite being innocent, Billy was blamed for the arrests.

Dean Watts was blinded in a vicious assault which took place in a nearby bar, when he approached the drunken lead singer of one of his favourite bands.

Laura Hickman's body was taken to a nearby park, soon after the clear up operation. She was stripped down and dumped in the middle of the night. With the government on the company's side, authorities were paid off to put the story out that she was the victim of a rape gone bad.

Jennifer Adams regained consciousness but was bedridden. She was unable to speak or move due to the damage sustained by the bullet. Nate Stephenson impressed his bosses by securing additional income for the company by renting her body out by the hour. Nate was also the driving force for the format change of the show, pioneering what was later screened as *The Game*.

The games continue.

Further reading:

Billy Smith's story continues in "Octopus 2" and "Under The Safe House"

Dean M. Watts and Steven Gibson's story continues in "Splattered Punk"

"The Game" and "The Game 2"

Author Bio

Matt Shaw is the author of over 200 published works. As well as appearing in a number of anthologies, Matt's work has been translated into French, German, Korean and Japanese. His work has also been adapted into graphic novels and - more recently - film.

Having successfully crowdfunded a feature film, in 2018 Matt Shaw adapted his best-selling novel MONSTER into a screenplay (with Shaun Hutson acting as script consultant) and then went on to direct it himself. The film starred Rod Glenn, Tracy Shaw (*Coronation Street*), Laura Ellen Wilson and Danielle Harold (*Eastenders*). Having broken his "film cherry", Matt is currently producing two more feature films - one an original piece which he wrote for screen (*Next Door*) and a second based on another of his novellas (*Love Life*).

Matt tours both the UK and the US on regular book signings but - if you're unable to get to where he is -

there is also a store where you can purchase signed merchandise direct from him over on ETSY. Simply look up *The Twisted World of Matt Shaw* where you'll find exclusive downloads, his infamous *DeadTed* bears and more…

Want to stay up to date with Matt? He can be found on Twitter, Instagram and Facebook. There is also a fan club which has exclusive stories, early reads, behind the scenes information and a whole lot more - available on Patreon!

Made in the USA
Columbia, SC
07 March 2020